Not that it Matters

A. A. Milne

Not that it Matters

Copyright © 2021 Bibliotech Press
All rights reserved

ISBN: 978-1-63637-469-7

CONTENTS

The Pleasure of Writing 1
Acacia Road 4
My Library 7
The Chase 11
Superstition 14
The Charm of Golf 17
Goldfish 20
Saturday to Monday 23
The Pond 26
A Seventeenth-century Story 29
Our Learned Friends 32
A Word for Autumn 36
A Christmas Number 39
No Flowers by Request 42
The Unfairness of Things 45
Daffodils 48
A Household Book 51
Lunch 54
The Friend of Man 57
The Diary Habit 60
Midsummer Day 63
At the Bookstall 66
"Who's Who" 69
A Day at Lord's 73
By the Sea 76
Golden Fruit 79
Signs of Character 82
Intellectual Snobbery 85
A Question of Form 88
A Slice of Fiction 91
The Label 94
The Profession 97
Smoking as a Fine Art 100

The Path to Glory 103

A Problem in Ethics 106

The Happiest Half-hours of Life 109

Natural Science 112

On Going Dry 115

A Misjudged Game 119

A Doubtful Character 123

Thoughts on Thermometers 126

For a Wet Afternoon 129

Declined with Thanks 132

On Going into a House 136

The Ideal Author 139

THE PLEASURE OF WRITING

Sometimes when the printer is waiting for an article which really should have been sent to him the day before, I sit at my desk and wonder if there is any possible subject in the whole world upon which I can possibly find anything to say. On one such occasion I left it to Fate, which decided, by means of a dictionary opened at random, that I should deliver myself of a few thoughts about goldfish. (You will find this article later on in the book.) But to-day I do not need to bother about a subject. To-day I am without a care. Nothing less has happened than that I have a new nib in my pen.

In the ordinary way, when Shakespeare writes a tragedy, or Mr. Blank gives you one of his charming little essays, a certain amount of thought goes on before pen is put to paper. One cannot write "Scene I. An Open Place. Thunder and Lightning. Enter Three Witches," or "As I look up from my window, the nodding daffodils beckon to me to take the morning," one cannot give of one's best in this way on the spur of the moment. At least, others cannot. But when I have a new nib in my pen, then I can go straight from my breakfast to the blotting-paper, and a new sheet of foolscap fills itself magically with a stream of blue-black words. When poets and idiots talk of the pleasure of writing, they mean the pleasure of giving a piece of their minds to the public; with an old nib a tedious business. They do not mean (as I do) the pleasure of the artist in seeing beautifully shaped "k's" and sinuous "s's" grow beneath his steel. Anybody else writing this article might wonder "Will my readers like it?" I only tell myself "How the compositors will love it!"

But perhaps they will not love it. Maybe I am a little above their heads. I remember on one First of January receiving an anonymous postcard wishing me a happy New Year, and suggesting that I should give the compositors a happy New Year also by writing more generously. In those days I got a thousand words upon one sheet 8 in. by 5 in. I adopted the suggestion, but it was a wrench; as it would be for a painter of miniatures forced to spend the rest of his life painting the Town Council of Boffington in the manner of Herkomer. My canvases are bigger now, but they are still impressionistic. "Pretty, but what is it?" remains the obvious comment; one steps back a pace and saws the air with the hand; "You see it better from here, my love," one says to one's wife. But if there be one compositor not carried away by the mad rush of life, who in a leisurely hour (the luncheon one, for instance) looks at the beautiful words with the eye of an artist, not of a wage-earner, he, I think, will be satisfied; he will be as glad as I am of my new nib. Does it matter, then, what you who see only the printed word think of it?

A woman, who had studied what she called the science of calligraphy, once offered to tell my character from my handwriting. I prepared a special sample for her; it was full of sentences like "To be good is to be happy," "Faith is the lode- star of life," "We should always be kind to animals," and so on. I wanted her to do her best. She gave the morning to it, and told me at lunch that I was "synthetic." Probably you think that the compositor has failed me here and printed "synthetic" when I wrote "sympathetic." In just this way I misunderstood my calligraphist at first, and I looked as sympathetic as I could. However, she repeated "synthetic," so that there could be no mistake. I begged her to tell me more, for I had thought that every letter would reveal a secret, but all she would add was "and not analytic." I went about for the rest of the day saying proudly to myself "I am synthetic! I am synthetic! I am synthetic!" and then I would add regretfully, "Alas, I am not analytic!" I had no idea what it meant.

And how do you think she had deduced my syntheticness? Simply from the fact that, to save time, I join some of my words together. That isn't being synthetic, it is being in a hurry. What she should have said was, "You are a busy man; your life is one constant whirl;

and probably you are of excellent moral character and kind to animals." Then one would feel that one did not write in vain.

My pen is getting tired; it has lost its first fair youth. However, I can still go on. I was at school with a boy whose uncle made nibs. If you detect traces of erudition in this article, of which any decent man might be expected to be innocent, I owe it to that boy. He once told me how many nibs his uncle made in a year; luckily I have forgotten. Thousands, probably. Every term that boy came back with a hundred of them; one expected him to be very busy. After all, if you haven't the brains or the inclination to work, it is something to have the nibs. These nibs, however, were put to better uses. There is a game you can play with them; you flick your nib against the other boy's nib, and if a lucky shot puts the head of yours under his, then a sharp tap capsizes him, and you have a hundred and one in your collection. There is a good deal of strategy in the game (whose finer points I have now forgotten), and I have no doubt that they play it at the Admiralty in the off season. Another game was to put a clean nib in your pen, place it lightly against the cheek of a boy whose head was turned away from you, and then call him suddenly. As Kipling says, we are the only really humorous race. This boy's uncle died a year or two later and left about £80,000, but none of it to his nephew. Of course, he had had the nibs every term. One mustn't forget that.

The nib I write this with is called the "Canadian Quill"; made, I suppose, from some steel goose which flourishes across the seas, and which Canadian housewives have to explain to their husbands every Michaelmas. Well, it has seen me to the end of what I wanted to say—if indeed I wanted to say anything. For it was enough for me this morning just to write; with spring coming in through the open windows and my good Canadian quill in my hand, I could have copied out a directory. That is the real pleasure of writing.

ACACIA ROAD

Of course there are disadvantages of suburban life. In the fourth act of the play there may be a moment when the fate of the erring wife hangs in the balance, and utterly regardless of this the last train starts from Victoria at 11.15. It must be annoying to have to leave her at such a crisis; it must be annoying too to have to preface the curtailed pleasures of the play with a meat tea and a hasty dressing in the afternoon. But, after all, one cannot judge life from its facilities for playgoing. It would be absurd to condemn the suburbs because of the 11.15.

There is a road eight miles from London up which I have walked sometimes on my way to golf. I think it is called Acacia Road; some pretty name like that. It may rain in Acacia Road, but never when I am there. The sun shines on Laburnum Lodge with its pink may tree, on the Cedars with its two clean limes, it casts its shadow on the ivy of Holly House, and upon the whole road there rests a pleasant afternoon peace. I cannot walk along Acacia Road without feeling that life could be very happy in it—when the sun is shining. It must be jolly, for instance, to live in Laburnum Lodge with its pink may tree. Sometimes I fancy that a suburban home is the true home after all.

When I pass Laburnum Lodge I think of Him saying good-bye to Her at the gate, as he takes the air each morning on his way to the station. What if the train is crowded? He has his newspaper. That will see him safely to the City. And then how interesting will be everything which happens to him there, since he has Her to tell it to when he comes home. The most ordinary street accident becomes exciting if a story has to be made of it. Happy the man who can say of each little incident, "I must remember to tell Her when I get home." And it is only in the suburbs that one "gets home." One does not "get home" to Grosvenor Square; one is simply "in" or "out."

But the master of Laburnum Lodge may have something better to tell his wife than the incident of the runaway horse; he may have heard a new funny story at lunch. The joke may have been all over the City, but it is unlikely that his wife in the suburbs will have heard it. Put it on the credit side of marriage that you can treasure up your jokes for some one else. And perhaps She has something for him too; some backward plant, it may be, has burst suddenly into flower; at least he will walk more eagerly up Acacia Road for wondering. So it will be a happy meeting under the pink may tree of Laburnum Lodge when these two are restored safely to each other after the excitements of the day. Possibly they will even do a little gardening together in the still glowing evening.

If life has anything more to offer than this it will be found at Holly House, where there are babies. Babies give an added excitement to the master's homecoming, for almost anything may have happened to them while he has been away. Dorothy perhaps has cut a new tooth and Anne may have said something really clever about the baker's man. In the morning, too, Anne will walk with him to the end of the road; it is perfectly safe, for in Acacia Road nothing untoward could occur. Even the dogs are quiet and friendly. I like to think of the master of Holly House saying good-bye to Anne at the end of the road and knowing that she will be alive when he comes back in the evening. That ought to make the day's work go quickly.

But it is the Cedars which gives us the secret of the happiness of the suburbs. The Cedars you observe is a grander house altogether; there is a tennis lawn at the back. And there are grown-up sons and daughters at the Cedars. In such houses in Acacia Road the delightful business of love-making is in full swing. Marriages are not "arranged" in the suburbs; they grow naturally out of the pleasant intercourse between the Cedars, the Elms, and Rose Bank. I see Tom walking over to the Elms, racket in hand, to play tennis with Miss Muriel. He is hoping for an invitation to remain to supper, and indeed I think he will get it. Anyhow he is going to ask Miss Muriel to come across to lunch to-morrow; his mother has so much to talk to her about. But it will be Tom who will do most of the talking.

I am sure that the marriages made in Acacia Road are happy. That is why I have no fears for Holly House and Laburnum Lodge. Of course they didn't make love in this Acacia Road; they are come from the Acacia Road of some other suburb, wisely deciding that they will be better away from their people. But they met each other in the same way as Tom and Muriel are meeting; He has seen Her in Her own home, in His home, at the tennis club, surrounded by the young bounders (confound them!) of Turret Court and the Wilderness; She has heard of him falling off his bicycle or quarrelling with his father. Bless you, they know all about each other; they are going to be happy enough together.

And now I think of it, why of course there is a local theatre where they can do their play- going, if they are as keen on it as that. For ten shillings they can spread from the stage box an air of luxury and refinement over the house; and they can nod in an easy manner across the stalls to the Cedars in the opposite box— in the deep recesses of which Tom and Muriel, you may be sure, are holding hands.

MY LIBRARY

When I moved into a new house a few weeks ago, my books, as was natural, moved with me. Strong, perspiring men shovelled them into packing-cases, and staggered with them to the van, cursing Caxton as they went. On arrival at this end, they staggered with them into the room selected for my library, heaved off the lids of the cases, and awaited orders. The immediate need was for an emptier room. Together we hurried the books into the new white shelves which awaited them, the order in which they stood being of no matter so long as they were off the floor. Armful after armful was hastily stacked, the only pause being when (in the curious way in which these things happen) my own name suddenly caught the eye of the foreman. "Did you write this one, sir?" he asked. I admitted it. "H'm," he said noncommittally. He glanced along the names of every armful after that, and appeared a little surprised at the number of books which I hadn't written. An easy-going profession, evidently.

So we got the books up at last, and there they are still. I told myself that when a wet afternoon came along I would arrange them properly. When the wet afternoon came, I told myself that I would arrange them one of these fine mornings. As they are now, I have to look along every shelf in the search for the book which I want. To come to Keats is no guarantee that we are on the road to Shelley. Shelley, if he did not drop out on the way, is probably next to How to Be a Golfer Though Middle-aged.

Having written as far as this, I had to get up and see where Shelley really was. It is worse than I thought. He is between Geometrical Optics and Studies in New Zealand Scenery. Ella Wheeler Wilcox, whom I find myself to be entertaining unawares, sits beside Anarchy or Order, which was apparently "sent in the hope that you will become a member of the Duty and Discipline Movement"—a vain hope, it would seem, for I have not yet paid my subscription. What I Found Out, by an English Governess, shares a corner with The Recreations of a Country Parson; they are followed by Villette and Baedeker's Switzerland. Something will have to be done about it. But I am wondering what is to be done. If I gave you the impression that my books were precisely arranged in their old shelves, I misled you. They were arranged in the order known as "all anyhow." Possibly they were a little less "anyhow" than they are now, in that the volumes of any particular work were at least together, but that is all that can be claimed for them. For years I put off the business of tidying them up, just as I am putting it off now. It is not laziness; it is simply that I don't know how to begin.

Let us suppose that we decide to have all the poetry together. It sounds reasonable. But then Byron is eleven inches high (my tallest poet), and Beattie (my shortest) is just over four inches. How foolish they will look standing side by side. Perhaps you don't know Beattie, but I assure you that he was a poet. He wrote those majestic lines: —

> "The shepherd-swain of whom I mention made
> On Scotia's mountains fed his little flock;
> The sickle, scythe or plough he never swayed —
> An honest heart was almost all his stock."

Of course, one would hardly expect a shepherd to sway a plough in the ordinary way, but Beattie was quite right to remind us that Edwin didn't either. Edwin was the name of the shepherd- swain. "And yet poor Edwin was no vulgar boy," we are told a little further on in a line that should live. Well, having satisfied you that Beattie was really a poet, I can now return to my argument that an eleven-inch Byron cannot stand next to a four-inch Beattie, and be followed by an eight-inch Cowper, without making the shelf look silly. Yet how can I discard Beattie— Beattie who wrote: —

> "And now the downy cheek and deepened voice
> Gave dignity to Edwin's blooming prime."

8

You see the difficulty. If you arrange your books according to their contents you are sure to get an untidy shelf. If you arrange your books according to their size and colour you get an effective wall, but the poetically inclined visitor may lose sight of Beattie altogether. Before, then, we decide what to do about it, we must ask ourselves that very awkward question, "Why do we have books on our shelves at all?" It is a most embarrassing question to answer.

Of course, you think that the proper answer (in your own case) is an indignant protest that you bought them in order to read them, and that yon put them on your shelves in order that you could refer to them when necessary. A little reflection will show you what a stupid answer that is. If you only want to read them, why are some of them bound in morocco and half-calf and other expensive coverings? Why did you buy a first edition when a hundredth edition was so much cheaper? Why have you got half a dozen copies of The Rubaiyat? What is the particular value of this other book that you treasure it so carefully? Why, the fact that its pages are uncut. If you cut the pages and read it, the value would go.

So, then, your library is not just for reference. You know as well as I do that it furnishes your room; that it furnishes it more effectively than does paint or mahogany or china. Of course, it is nice to have the books there, so that one can refer to them when one wishes. One may be writing an article on sea-bathing, for instance, and have come to the sentence which begins: "In the well-remembered words of Coleridge, perhaps almost too familiar to be quoted"—and then one may have to look them up. On these occasions a library is not only ornamental but useful. But do not let us be ashamed that we find it ornamental. Indeed, the more I survey it, the more I feel that my library is sufficiently ornamental as it stands. Any reassembling of the books might spoil the colour-scheme. Baedeker's Switzerland and Villette are both in red, a colour which is neatly caught up again, after an interlude in blue, by a volume of Browning and Jevons' Elementary Logic. We had a woman here only yesterday who said, "How pretty your books look," and I am inclined to think that that is good enough. There is a careless rapture about them which I should lose if I started to arrange them methodically.

But perhaps I might risk this to the extent of getting all their heads the same way up. Yes, on one of these fine days (or wet nights) I shall take my library seriously in hand. There are still one or two books which are the wrong way round. I shall put them the right way round.

THE CHASE

The fact, as revealed in a recent lawsuit, that there is a gentleman in this country who spends £10,000 a year upon his butterfly collection would have disturbed me more in the early nineties than it does to-day. I can bear it calmly now, but twenty-five years ago the knowledge would have spoilt my pride in my own collection, upon which I was already spending the best part of threepence a week pocket-money. Perhaps, though, I should have consoled myself with the thought that I was the truer enthusiast of the two; for when my rival hears of a rare butterfly in Brazil, he sends a man out to Brazil to capture it, whereas I, when I heard that there was a Clouded Yellow in the garden, took good care that nobody but myself encompassed its death. Our aims also were different. I purposely left Brazil out of it.

Whether butterfly-hunting is good or bad for the character I cannot undertake to decide. No doubt it can be justified as clearly as fox-hunting. If the fox eats chickens, the butterfly's child eats vegetables; if fox-hunting improves the breed of horses, butterfly-hunting improves the health of boys. But at least, we never told ourselves that butterflies liked being pursued, as (I understand) foxes like being hunted. We were moderately honest about it. And we comforted ourselves in the end with the assurance of many eminent naturalists that "insects don't feel pain."

I have often wondered how naturalists dare to speak with such authority. Do they never have dreams at night of an after-life in some other world, wherein they are pursued by giant insects eager to increase their "naturalist collection"—insects who assure each other carelessly that "naturalists don't feel pain"? Perhaps they do so dream. But we, at any rate, slept well, for we had never dogmatized about a butterfly's feelings. We only quoted the wise men.

11

But if there might be doubt about the sensitiveness of a butterfly, there could be no doubt about his distinguishing marks. It was amazing to us how many grown-up and (presumably) educated men and women did not know that a butterfly had knobs on the end of his antennae, and that the moth had none. Where had they been all these years to be so ignorant? Well-meaning but misguided aunts, with mysterious promises of a new butterfly for our collection, would produce some common Yellow Underwing from an envelope, innocent (for which they may be forgiven) that only a personal capture had any value to us, but unforgivably ignorant that a Yellow Underwing was a moth. We did not collect moths; there were too many of them. And moths are nocturnal creatures. A hunter whose bed-time depends upon the whim of another is handicapped for the night-chase.

But butterflies come out when the sun comes out, which is just when little boys should be out; and there are not too many butterflies in England. I knew them all by name once, and could have recognized any that I saw—yes, even Hampstead's Albion Eye (or was it Albion's Hampstead Eye?), of which only one specimen had ever been caught in this country; presumably by Hampstead— or Albion. In my day-dreams the second specimen was caught by me. Yet he was an insignificant-looking fellow, and perhaps I should have been better pleased with a Camberwell Beauty, a Purple Emperor, or a Swallowtail. Unhappily the Purple Emperor (so the book told us) haunted the tops of trees, which was to take an unfair advantage of a boy small for his age, and the Swallowtail haunted Norfolk, which was equally inconsiderate of a family which kept holiday in the south. The Camberwell Beauty sounded more hopeful, but I suppose the trams disheartened him. I doubt if he ever haunted Camberwell in my time.

With threepence a week one has to be careful. It was necessary to buy killing-boxes and setting-boards, but butterfly-nets could be made at home. A stick, a piece of copper wire, and some muslin were all that were necessary. One liked the muslin to be green, for there was a feeling that this deceived the butterfly in some way; he

12

thought that Birnam Wood was merely coming to Dunsinane when he saw it approaching, and that the queer-looking thing behind was some local efflorescence. So he resumed his dalliance with the herbaceous border, and was never more surprised in his life than when it turned out to be a boy and a butterfly-net. Green muslin, then, but a plain piece of cane for the stick. None of your collapsible fishing-rods—"suitable for a Purple Emperor." Leave those to the millionaire's sons.

It comes back to me now that I am doing this afternoon what I did more than twenty-five years ago; I am writing an article upon the way to make a butterfly-net. For my first contribution to the press was upon this subject. I sent it to the editor of some boys' paper, and his failure to print it puzzled me a good deal, since every word in it (I was sure) was correctly spelt. Of course, I see now that you want more in an article than that. But besides being puzzled I was extremely disappointed, for I wanted badly the money that it should have brought in. I wanted it in order to buy a butterfly-net; the stick and the copper wire and the green muslin being (in my hands, at any rate) more suited to an article.

SUPERSTITION

I have just read a serious column on the prospects for next year. This article consisted of contributions from experts in the various branches of industry (including one from a meteorological expert who, I need hardly tell you, forecasted a wet summer) and ended with a general summing up of the year by Old Moore or one of the minor prophets. Old Moore, I am sorry to say, left me cold.

I should like to believe in astrology, but I cannot. I should like to believe that the heavenly bodies sort themselves into certain positions in order that Zadkiel may be kept in touch with the future; the idea of a star whizzing a million miles out of its path by way of indicating a "sensational divorce case in high life" is extraordinarily massive. But, candidly, I do not believe the stars bother. What the stars are for, what they are like when you get there, I do not know; but a starry night would not be so beautiful if it were simply meant as a warning to some unpleasant financier that Kaffirs were going up. The ordinary man looks at the heavens and thinks what an insignificant atom he is beneath them; the believer in astrology looks up and realizes afresh his overwhelming importance. Perhaps, after all, I am glad I do not believe.

Life must be a very tricky thing for the superstitious. At dinner a night or two ago I happened to say that I had never been in danger of drowning. I am not sure now that it was true, but I still think that it was harmless. However, before I had time to elaborate my theme (whatever it was) I was peremptorily ordered to touch wood. I protested that both my feet were on the polished oak and both my elbows on the polished mahogany (one always knew that some good instinct inspired the pleasant habit of elbows on the table) and that anyhow I did not see the need. However, because one must not argue at dinner I tapped the table two or three times... and now I suppose I am immune. At the same time I should like to know exactly whom I have appeased.

For this must be the idea of the wood-touching superstition, that a malignant spirit dogs one's conversational footsteps, listening eagerly for the complacent word. "I have never had the mumps," you say airily. "Ha, ha!" says the spirit, "haven't you? Just you wait till next Tuesday, my boy." Unconsciously we are crediting Fate with our own human weaknesses. If a man standing on the edge of a pond said aloud, "I have never fallen into a pond in my life," and we happened to be just behind him, the temptation to push him in would be irresistible. Irresistible, that is by us; but it is charitable to assume that Providence can control itself by now.

Of course, nobody really thinks that our good or evil spirits have any particular feeling about wood, that they like it stroked; nobody, I suppose, not even the most superstitious, really thinks that Fate is especially touchy in the matter of salt and ladders. Equally, of course, many people who throw spilt salt over their left shoulders are not superstitious in the least, and are only concerned to display that readiness in the face of any social emergency which is said to be the mark of good manners. But there are certainly many who feel that it is the part of a wise man to propitiate the unknown, to bend before the forces which work for harm; and they pay tribute to Fate by means of these little customs in the hope that they will secure in return an immunity from evil. The tribute is nominal, but it is an acknowledgment all the same.

A proper sense of proportion leaves no room for superstition. A man says, "I have never been in a shipwreck," and becoming nervous touches wood. Why is he nervous? He has this paragraph before his eyes: "Among the deceased was Mr. — —. By a remarkable coincidence this gentleman had been saying only a few days before that he had never been in a shipwreck. Little did he think that his next voyage would falsify his words so tragically." It occurs to him that he has read paragraphs like that again and again. Perhaps he has. Certainly he has never read a paragraph like this:

"Among the deceased was Mr. — —. By a remarkable coincidence this gentleman had never made the remark that he had not yet been in a shipwreck." Yet that paragraph could have been written truthfully thousands of times. A sense of proportion would tell you that, if only one side of a case is ever recorded, that side acquires an undue importance. The truth is that Fate does not go out of its way to be dramatic. If you or I had the power of life and death in our hands, we should no doubt arrange some remarkably bright and telling effects. A man who spilt the salt callously would be drowned next week in the Dead Sea, and a couple who married in May would expire simultaneously in the May following. But Fate cannot worry to think out all the clever things that we should think out. It goes about its business solidly and unromantically, and by the ordinary laws of chance it achieves every now and then something startling and romantic. Superstition thrives on the fact that only the accidental dramas are reported.

But there are charms to secure happiness as well as charms to avert evil. In these I am a firm believer. I do not mean that I believe that a horseshoe hung up in the house will bring me good luck; I mean that if anybody does believe this, then the hanging up of his horseshoe will probably bring him good luck. For if you believe that you are going to be lucky, you go about your business with a smile, you take disaster with a smile, you start afresh with a smile. And to do that is to be in the way of happiness.

THE CHARM OF GOLF

When he reads of the notable doings of famous golfers, the eighteen-handicap man has no envy in his heart. For by this time he has discovered the great secret of golf. Before he began to play he wondered wherein lay the fascination of it; now he knows. Golf is so popular simply because it is the best game in the world at which to be bad.

Consider what it is to be bad at cricket. You have bought a new bat, perfect in balance; a new pair of pads, white as driven snow; gloves of the very latest design. Do they let you use them? No. After one ball, in the negotiation of which neither your bat, nor your pads, nor your gloves came into play, they send you back into the pavilion to spend the rest of the afternoon listening to fatuous stories of some old gentleman who knew Fuller Pilch. And when your side takes the field, where are you? Probably at long leg both ends, exposed to the public gaze as the worst fieldsman in London. How devastating are your emotions. Remorse, anger, mortification, fill your heart; above all, envy—envy of the lucky immortals who disport themselves on the green level of Lord's.

Consider what it is to be bad at lawn tennis. True, you are allowed to hold on to your new racket all through the game, but how often are you allowed to employ it usefully? How often does your partner cry "Mine!" and bundle you out of the way? Is there pleasure in playing football badly? You may spend the full eighty minutes in your new boots, but your relations with the ball will be distant. They do not give you a ball to yourself at football.

But how different a game is golf. At golf it is the bad player who gets the most strokes. However good his opponent, the bad player has the right to play out each hole to the end; he will get more than his share of the game. He need have no fears that his new driver will not be employed. He will have as many swings with it as the scratch man; more, if he misses the ball altogether upon one or two tees. If he buys a new niblick he is certain to get fun out of it on the very first day.

And, above all, there is this to be said for golfing mediocrity— the bad player can make the strokes of the good player. The poor cricketer has perhaps never made fifty in his life; as soon as he stands at the wickets he knows that he is not going to make fifty to-day. But the eighteen-handicap man has some time or other played every hole on the course to perfection. He has driven a ball 250 yards; he has made superb approaches; he has run down the long putt. Any of these things may suddenly happen to him again. And therefore it is not his fate to have to sit in the club smoking- room after his second round and listen to the wonderful deeds of others. He can join in too. He can say with perfect truth, "I once carried the ditch at the fourth with my second," or "I remember when I drove into the bunker guarding the eighth green," or even "I did a three at the eleventh this afternoon"—bogey being five. But if the bad cricketer says, "I remember when I took a century in forty minutes off Lockwood and Richardson," he is nothing but a liar.

For these and other reasons golf is the best game in the world for the bad player. And sometimes I am tempted to go further and say that it is a better game for the bad player than for the good player. The joy of driving a ball straight after a week of slicing, the joy of putting a mashie shot dead, the joy of even a moderate stroke with a brassie; best of all, the joy of the perfect cleek shot—these things the good player will never know. Every stroke we bad players make we make in hope. It is never so bad but it might have been worse; it is never so bad but we are confident of doing better next time. And if the next stroke is good, what happiness fills our soul. How eagerly we tell ourselves that in a little while all our strokes will be as good.

What does Vardon know of this? If he does a five hole in four he blames himself that he did not do it in three; if he does it in five he is miserable. He will never experience that happy surprise with which we hail our best strokes. Only his bad strokes surprise him, and then we may suppose that he is not happy. His length and accuracy are mechanical; they are not the result, as so often in our case, of some suddenly applied maxim or some suddenly discovered innovation. The only thing which can vary in his game is his putting, and putting is not golf but croquet.

But of course we, too, are going to be as good as Vardon one day. We are only postponing the day because meanwhile it is so pleasant to be bad. And it is part of the charm of being bad at golf that in a moment, in a single night, we may become good. If the bad cricketer said to a good cricketer, "What am I doing wrong?" the only possible answer would be, "Nothing particular, except that you can't play cricket." But if you or I were to say to our scratch friend, "What am I doing wrong?" he would reply at once, "Moving the head" or "Dropping the right knee" or "Not getting the wrists in soon enough," and by to-morrow we should be different players. Upon such a little depends, or seems to the eighteen-handicap to depend, excellence in golf.

And so, perfectly happy in our present badness and perfectly confident of our future goodness, we long-handicap men remain. Perhaps it would be pleasanter to be a little more certain of getting the ball safely off the first tee; perhaps at the fourteenth hole, where there is a right of way and the public encroach, we should like to feel that we have done with topping; perhaps—

Well, perhaps we might get our handicap down to fifteen this summer. But no lower; certainly no lower.

GOLDFISH

Let us talk about—well, anything you will. Goldfish, for instance.

Goldfish are a symbol of old-world tranquillity or mid-Victorian futility according to their position in the home. Outside the home, in that wild state from which civilization has dragged them, they may have stood for dare-devil courage or constancy or devotion; I cannot tell. I may only speak of them now as I find them, which is in the garden or in the drawing-room. In their lily-leaved pool, sunk deep in the old flagged terrace, upon whose borders the blackbird whistles his early-morning song, they remind me of sundials and lavender and old delightful things. But in their cheap glass bowl upon the three- legged table, above which the cloth-covered canary maintains a stolid silence, they remind me of antimacassars and horsehair sofas and all that is depressing. It is hard that the goldfish himself should have so little choice in the matter. Goldfish look pretty in the terrace pond, yet I doubt if it was the need for prettiness which brought them there. Rather the need for some thing to throw things to. No one of the initiate can sit in front of Nature's most wonderful effect, the sea, without wishing to throw stones into it, the physical pleasure of the effort and the aesthetic pleasure of the splash combining to produce perfect contentment. So by the margin of the pool the same desires stir within one, and because ants' eggs do not splash, and look untidy on the surface of the water, there must be a gleam of gold and silver to put the crown upon one's pleasure.

Perhaps when you have been feeding the goldfish you have not thought of it like that. But at least you must have wondered why, of all diets, they should prefer ants' eggs. Ants' eggs are, I should say, the very last thing which one would take to without argument. It must be an acquired taste, and, this being so, one naturally asks oneself how goldfish came to acquire it.

I suppose (but I am lamentably ignorant on these as on all other matters) that there was a time when goldfish lived a wild free life of their own. They roamed the sea or the river, or whatever it was, fighting for existence, and Nature showed them, as she always does, the food which suited them. Now I have often come across ants' nests in my travels, but never when swimming. In seas and rivers, pools and lakes, I have wandered, but Nature has never put ants' eggs in my way. No doubt—it would be only right- -the goldfish has a keener eye than I have for these things, but if they had been there, should I have missed them so completely? I think not, for if they had been there, they must have been there in great quantities. I can imagine a goldfish slowly acquiring the taste for them through the centuries, but only if other food were denied to him, only if, wherever he went, ants' eggs, ants' eggs, ants' eggs drifted down the stream to him.

Yet, since it would seem that he has acquired the taste, it can only be that the taste has come to him with captivity—has been forced upon him, I should have said. The old wild goldfish (this is my theory) was a more terrible beast than we think. Given his proper diet, he could not have been kept within the limits of the terrace pool. He would have been unsuited to domestic life; he would have dragged in the shrieking child as she leant to feed him. As the result of many experiments ants' eggs were given him to keep him thin (you can see for yourself what a bloodless diet it is), ants' eggs were given him to quell his spirit; and just as a man, if he has sufficient colds, can get up a passion even for ammoniated quinine, so the goldfish has grown in captivity to welcome the once-hated omelette.

Let us consider now the case of the goldfish in the house. His diet is the same, but how different his surroundings! If his bowl is placed on a table in the middle of the floor, he has but to flash his tail once and he has been all round the drawing-room. The drawing-room may not seem much to you, but to him this impressionist picture through the curved glass must be amazing. Let not the outdoor goldfish boast of his freedom. What does he, in his little world of

21

water-lily roots, know of the vista upon vista which opens to his more happy brother as he passes jauntily from china dog to ottoman and from ottoman to Henry's father? Ah, here is life! It may be that in the course of years he will get used to it, even bored by it; indeed, for that reason I always advocate giving him a glance at the dining-room or the bedrooms on Wednesdays and Saturdays; but his first day in the bowl must be the opening of an undreamt of heaven to him.

Again, what an adventurous life is his. At any moment a cat may climb up and fetch him out, a child may upset him, grown-ups may neglect to feed him or to change his water. The temptation to take him up and massage him must be irresistible to outsiders. All these dangers the goldfish in the pond avoids; he lives a sheltered and unexciting life, and when he wants to die he dies unnoticed, unregretted, but for his brother the tears and the solemn funeral.

Yes; now that I have thought it out, I can see that I was wrong in calling the indoor goldfish a symbol of mid-Victorian futility. An article of this sort is no good if it does not teach the writer something as well as his readers. I recognize him now as the symbol of enterprise and endurance, of restlessness and Post-Impressionism. He is not mid-Victorian, he is Fifth Georgian.

Which is all I want to say about goldfish.

SATURDAY TO MONDAY

The happy man would have happy faces round him; a sad face is a reproach to him for his happiness. So when I escape by the 2.10 on Saturday I distribute largesse with a liberal hand. The cabman, feeling that an effort is required of him, mentions that I am the first gentleman he has met that day; he penetrates my mufti and calls me captain, leaving it open whether he regards me as a Salvation Army captain or the captain of a barge. The porters hasten to the door of my cab; there is a little struggle between them as to who shall have the honour of waiting upon me. ...

Inside the station things go on as happily. The booking-office clerk gives me a pleasant smile; he seems to approve of the station I am taking. "Some do go to Brighton," he implies, "but for a gentleman like you—" He pauses to point out that with this ticket I can come back on the Tuesday if I like (as, between ourselves, I hope to do). In exchange for his courtesies I push him my paper through the pigeon hole. A dirty little boy thrust it into my cab; I didn't want it, but as we are all being happy to- day he had his penny.

I follow my porter to the platform. "On the left," says the ticket collector. He has said it mechanically to a hundred persons, but he becomes human and kindly as he says it to me. I feel that he really wishes me to get into the right train, to have a pleasant journey down, to be welcomed heartily by my friends when I arrive. It is not as to one of a mob but to an individual that he speaks.

The porter has found me an empty carriage. He is full of ideas for my comfort; he tells me which way the train will start, where we stop, and when we may be expected to arrive. Am I sure I wouldn't like my bag in the van? Can he get me any papers? No; no, thanks. I don't want to read. I give him sixpence, and there is another one of us happy.

Presently the guard. He also seems pleased that I have selected this one particular station from among so many. Pleased, but not astonished; he expected it of me. It is a very good run down in his train, and he shouldn't be surprised if we had a fine week- end. ...

I stand at the door of ray carriage feeling very happy. It is good to get out of London. Come to think of it, we are all getting out of London, and none of us is going to do any work to- morrow. How jolly! Oh, but what about my porter? Bother! I wish now I'd given him more than sixpence. Still, he may have a sweetheart and be happy that way.

We are off. I have nothing to read, but then I want to think. It is the ideal place in which to think, a railway carriage; the ideal place in which to be happy. I wonder if I shall be in good form this week-end at cricket and tennis, and croquet and billiards, and all the other jolly games I mean to play. Look at those children trying to play cricket in that dirty backyard. Poor little beggars! Fancy living in one of those horrible squalid houses. But you cannot spoil to- day for me, little backyards. On Tuesday perhaps, when I am coming again to the ugly town, your misery will make me miserable; I shall ask myself hopelessly what it all means; but just now I am too happy for pity. After all, why should I assume that you envy me, you two children swinging on a gate and waving to me? You are happy, aren't you? Of course; we are all happy to-day. See, I am waving back to you.

My eyes wander round the carriage and rest on my bag. Have I put everything in? Of course I have. Then why this uneasy feeling that I have left something very important out? Well, I can soon settle the question. Let's start with to-night. Evening clothes— they're in, I know. Shirts, collars ...

I go through the whole programme for the week-end, allotting myself in my mind suitable clothes for each occasion. Yes; I seem to have brought everything that I can possibly want. But what a very jolly programme I am drawing up for myself! Will it really be as delightful as that? Well, it was last time, and the time before; that is why I am so happy.

The train draws up at its only halt in the glow of a September mid-afternoon. There is a little pleasant bustle; nice people get out and nice people meet them; everybody seems very cheery and contented. Then we are off again ... and now the next station is mine.

We are there. A porter takes my things with a kindly smile and a "Nice day." I see Brant outside with the wagonette, not the trap; then I am not the only guest coming by this train. Who are the others, I wonder. Anybody I know? ... Why, yes, it's Bob and Mrs. Bob, and—hallo!—Cynthia! And isn't that old Anderby? How splendid! I must get that shilling back from Bob that I lost to him at billiards last time. And if Cynthia really thinks that she can play croquet ...

We greet each other happily and climb into the wagonette. Never has the country looked so lovely. "No; no rain at all," says Brant, "and the glass is going up." The porter puts our luggage in the cart and comes round with a smile. It is a rotten life being a porter, and I do so want everybody to enjoy this afternoon. Besides, I haven't any coppers.

I slip half a crown into his palm. Now we are all very, very happy.

THE POND

My friend Aldenham's pond stands at a convenient distance from the house, and is reached by a well-drained gravel path; so that in any weather one may walk, alone or in company, dry shod to its brink, and estimate roughly how many inches of rain have fallen in the night. The ribald call it the hippopotamus pond, tracing a resemblance between it and the bath of the hippopotamus at the Zoo, beneath the waters of which, if you particularly desire to point the hippopotamus out to somebody, he always lies hidden. To the rest of us it is known simply as "the pond"—a designation which ignores the existence of several neighbouring ponds, the gifts of nature, and gives the whole credit to the handiwork of man. For "the pond" is just a small artificial affair of cement, entirely unpretentious.

There are seven steps to the bottom of the pond, and each step is 10 in. high. Thus the steps help to make the pond a convenient rain-gauge; for obviously when only three steps are left uncovered, as was the case last Monday, you know that there have been 40 in. of rain since last month, when the pond began to fill. To strangers this may seem surprising, and it is only fair to tell them the great secret, which is that much of the surrounding land drains secretly into the pond too. This seems to me to give a much fairer indication of the rain that has fallen than do the official figures in the newspapers. For when your whole day's cricket has been spoilt, it is perfectly absurd to be told that .026 of an inch of rain has done the damage; the soul yearns for something more startling than that The record of the pond, that there has been another 5 in., soothes us, where the record of the ordinary pedantic rain-gauge would leave us infuriated. It speaks much for my friend Aldenham's breadth of view that he understood this, and planned the pond accordingly.

A most necessary thing in a country house is that there should be a recognized meeting-place, where the people who have been writing a few letters after breakfast may, when they have finished, meet those who have no intention of writing any, and arrange plans with them for the morning. I am one of those who cannot write letters in another man's house, and when my pipe is well alight I say to Miss Robinson—or whoever it may be—"Let's go and look at the pond." "Right oh," she says willingly enough, having spent the last quarter of an hour with The Times Financial Supplement, all of the paper that is left to the women in the first rush for the cricket news. We wander down to the pond together, and perhaps find Brown and Miss Smith there. "A lot of rain in the night," says Brown. "It was only just over the third step after lunch yesterday." We have a little argument about it, Miss Robinson being convinced that she stood on the second step after breakfast, and Miss Smith repeating that it looks exactly the same to her this morning. By and by two or three others stroll up, and we all make measurements together. The general opinion is that there has been a lot of rain in the night, and that 43 in. in three weeks must be a record. But, anyhow, it is fairly fine now, and what about a little lawn tennis? Or golf? Or croquet? Or—? And so the arrangements for the morning are made.

And they can be made more readily out of doors; for—supposing it is fine—the fresh air calls you to be doing something, and the sight of the newly marked tennis lawn fills you with thoughts of revenge for your accidental defeat the evening before. But indoors it is so easy to drop into a sofa after breakfast, and, once there with all the papers, to be disinclined to leave it till lunch-time. A man or woman as lazy as this must not be rushed. Say to such a one, "Come and play," and the invitation will be declined. Say, "Come and look at the pond," and the worst sluggard will not refuse such gentle exercise. And once he is out he is out.

All this for those delightful summer days when there are fine intervals; but consider the advantages of the pond when the rain streams down in torrents from morning till night. How tired we get of being indoors on these days, even with the best of books, the pleasantest of companions, the easiest of billiard tables. Yet if our hostess were to see us marching out with an umbrella, how odd she would think us. "Where are you off to?" she would ask, and we could only answer lamely, "Er—I was just going to— er—walk about a bit." But now we tell her brightly, "I'm going to see the pond. It must be nearly full. Won't you come too?" And with any luck she comes. And you know, it even reconciles us a little to these streaming days to reflect that it all goes to fill the pond. For there is ever before our minds that great moment in the future when the pond is at last full. What will happen then? Aldenham may know, but we his guests do not. Some think there will be merely a flood over the surrounding paths and the kitchen garden, but for myself I believe that we are promised something much bigger than that. A man with such a broad and friendly outlook towards rain-gauges will be sure to arrange something striking when the great moment arrives. Some sort of fete will help to celebrate it, I have no doubt; with an open-air play, tank drama, or what not. At any rate we have every hope that he will empty the pond as speedily as possible so that we may watch it fill again.

I must say that he has been a little lucky in his choice of a year for inaugurating the pond. But, all the same, there are now 45 in. of rain in it, 45 in. of rain have fallen in the last three weeks, and I think that something ought to be done about it.

A SEVENTEENTH-CENTURY STORY

There is a story in every name in that first column of The Times- - Births, Marriages, and Deaths—down which we glance each morning, but, unless the name is known to us, we do not bother about the stories of other people. They are those not very interesting people, our contemporaries. But in a country churchyard a name on an old tombstone will set us wondering a little. What sort of life came to an end there a hundred years ago?

In the parish register we shall find the whole history of them; when they were born, when they were married, how many children they had, when they died—a skeleton of their lives which we can clothe with our fancies and make living again. Simple lives, we make them, in that pleasant countryside; "Man comes and tills the field and lies beneath"; that is all. Simple work, simple pleasures, and a simple death.

Of course we are wrong. There were passions and pains in those lives; tragedies perhaps. The tombstones and the registers say nothing of them; or, if they say it, it is in a cypher to which we have not the key. Yet sometimes the key is almost in our hands. Here is a story from the register of a village church— four entries only, but they hide a tragedy which with a little imagination we can almost piece together for ourselves.

The first entry is a marriage. John Meadowes of Littlehaw Manor, bachelor, took Mary Field to wife (both of this parish) on 7th November 1681.

There were no children of the marriage. Indeed, it only lasted a year. A year later, on 12th November 1682, John died and was buried.

Poor Mary Meadowes was now alone at the Manor. We picture her sitting there in her loneliness, broken-hearted, refusing to be comforted. ...

Until we come to the third entry. John has only been in his grave a month, but here is the third entry, telling us that on 12th December 1682, Robert Cliff, bachelor, was married to Mary Meadowes, widow. It spoils our picture of her. ...

And then the fourth entry. It is the fourth entry which reveals the tragedy, which makes us wonder what is the story hidden away in the parish register of Littlehaw—the mystery of Littlehaw Manor. For here is another death, the death of Mary Cliff, and Mary Cliff died on ... 13th December 1682.

And she was buried in unconsecrated ground. For Mary Cliff (we must suppose) had killed herself. She had killed herself on the day after her marriage to her second husband.

Well, what is the story? We shall have to make it up for ourselves. Here is my rendering of it. I have no means of finding out if it is the correct one, but it seems to fit itself within the facts as we know them.

Mary Field was the daughter of well-to-do parents, an only child, and the most desirable bride, from the worldly point of view, in the village. No wonder, then, that her parents' choice of a husband for her fell upon the most desirable bridegroom of the village—John Meadowes. The Fields' land adjoined Littlehaw Manor; one day the child of John and Mary would own it all. Let a marriage, then, be arranged.

But Mary loved Robert Cliff whole-heartedly —Robert, a man of no standing at all. A ridiculous notion, said her parents, but the silly girl would grow out of it. She was taken by a handsome face. Once she was safely wedded to John, she would forget her foolishness. John might not be handsome, but he was a solid, steady fellow; which was more—much more, as it turned out—than could be said for Robert.

30

So John and Mary married. But she still loved Robert. ...

Did she kill her husband? Did she and Robert kill him together? Or did she only hasten his death by her neglect of him in some illness? Did she dare him to ride some devil of a horse which she knew he could not master; did she taunt him into some foolhardy feat; or did she deliberately kill him—with or without her lover's aid? I cannot guess, but of this I am certain. His death was on her conscience. Directly or indirectly she was responsible for it —or, at any rate, felt herself responsible for it. But she would not think of it too closely; she had room for only one thought in her mind. She was mistress of Littlehaw Manor now, and free to marry whom she wished. Free, at last, to marry Robert. Whatever had been done had been worth doing for that.

So she married him. And then—so I read the story—she discovered the truth. Robert had never loved her. He had wanted to marry the rich Miss Field, that was all. Still more, he had wanted to marry the rich Mrs. Meadowes. He was quite callous about it. She might as well know the truth now as later. It would save trouble in the future, if she knew.

So Mary killed herself. She had murdered John for nothing. Whatever her responsibility for John's death, in the bitterness of that discovery she would call it murder. She had a murder on her conscience for love's sake—and there was no love. What else to do but follow John? ...

Is that the story? I wonder.

OUR LEARNED FRIENDS

I do not know why the Bar has always seemed the most respectable of the professions, a profession which the hero of almost any novel could adopt without losing caste. But so it is. A schoolmaster can be referred to contemptuously as an usher; a doctor is regarded humorously as a licensed murderer; a solicitor is always retiring to gaol for making away with trust funds, and, in any case, is merely an attorney; while a civil servant sleeps from ten to four every day, and is only waked up at sixty in order to be given a pension. But there is no humorous comment to be made upon the barrister—unless it is to call him "my learned friend." He has much more right than the actor to claim to be a member of the profession. I don't know why. Perhaps it is because he walks about the Temple in a top-hat.

So many of one's acquaintances at some time or other have "eaten dinners" that one hardly dares to say anything against the profession. Besides, one never knows when one may not want to be defended. However, I shall take the risk, and put the barrister in the dock. "Gentlemen of the jury, observe this well-dressed gentleman before you. What shall we say about him?"

Let us begin by asking ourselves what we expect from a profession. In the first place, certainly, we expect a living, but I think we want something more than that. If we were offered a thousand a year to walk from Charing Cross to Barnet every day, reasons of poverty might compel us to accept the offer, but we should hardly be proud of our new profession. We should prefer to earn a thousand a year by doing some more useful work. Indeed, to a man of any fine feeling the profession of Barnet walking would only be tolerable if he could persuade himself that by his exertions he was helping to revive the neglected art of pedestrianism, or to make more popular the neglected beauties of Barnet; if he could hope that, after his three- hundredth journey, inquisitive people would begin to follow him, wondering what he was after, and so come suddenly upon the old Norman church at the cross-roads, or, if they missed this, at any rate upon a much better appetite for their dinner. That is to say, he would have to persuade himself that he was walking, not only for himself, but also for the community.

It seems to me, then, that a profession is a noble or an ignoble one, according as it offers or denies to him who practises it the opportunity of working for some other end than his own advancement. A doctor collects fees from his patients, but he is aiming at something more than pounds, shillings, and pence; he is out to put an end to suffering. A schoolmaster earns a living by teaching, but he does not feel that he is fighting only for himself; he is a crusader on behalf of education. The artist, whatever his medium, is giving a message to the world, expressing the truth as he sees it; for his own profit, perhaps, but not for that alone. All these and a thousand other ways of living have something of nobility in them. We enter them full of high resolves. We tell ourselves that we will follow the light as it has been revealed to us; that our ideals shall never be lowered; that we will refuse to sacrifice our principles to our interests. We fail, of course. The painter finds that "Mother's Darling" brings in the stuff, and he turns out Mother's Darlings mechanically. The doctor neglects research and cultivates instead a bedside manner. The schoolmaster drops all his theories of education and conforms hastily to those of his employers. We fail, but it is not because the profession is an ignoble one; we had our chances. Indeed, the light is still there for those who look. It beckons to us.

Now what of the Bar? Is the barrister after anything other than his own advancement? He follows what gleam? What are his ideals? Never mind whether he fails more often or less often than others to attain them; I am not bothering about that. I only want to know what it is that he is after. In the quiet hours when we are alone with ourselves and there is nobody to tell us what fine fellows we are, we come sometimes upon a weak moment in which we wonder,

33

not how much money we are earning, nor how famous we are becoming, but what good we are doing. If a barrister ever has such a moment, what is his consolation? It can only be that he is helping Justice to be administered. If he is to be proud of his profession, and in that lonely moment tolerant of himself, he must feel that he is taking a noble part in the vindication of legal right, the punishment of legal wrong. But he must do more than this. Just as the doctor, with increased knowledge and experience, becomes a better fighter against disease, advancing himself, no doubt, but advancing also medical science; just as the schoolmaster, having learnt new and better ways of teaching, can now give a better education to his boys, increasing thereby the sum of knowledge; so the barrister must be able to tell himself that the more expert he becomes as an advocate, the better will he be able to help in the administration of this Justice which is his ideal.

Can he tell himself this? I do not see how he can. His increased expertness will be of increased service to himself, of increased service to his clients, but no ideal will be the better served by reason of it. Let us take a case—Smith v. Jones. Counsel is briefed for Smith. After examining the case he tells himself in effect this: "As far as I can see, the Law is all on the other side. Luckily, however, sentiment is on our side. Given an impressionable jury, there's just a chance that we might pull it off. It's worth trying." He tries, and if he is sufficiently expert he pulls it off. A triumph for himself, but what has happened to the ideal? Did he even think, "Of course I'm bound to do the best for my client, but he's in the wrong, and I hope we lose?" I imagine not. The whole teaching of the Bar is that he must not bother about justice, but only about his own victory. What ultimately, then, is he after? What does the Bar offer its devotees— beyond material success?

I asked just now what were a barrister's ideals. Suppose we ask instead, What is the ideal barrister? If one spoke loosely of an ideal doctor, one would not necessarily mean a titled gentleman in Harley Street. An ideal schoolmaster is not synonymous with the Headmaster of Eton or the owner of the most profitable preparatory school. But can there be an ideal barrister other than a successful barrister? The eager young writer, just beginning a literary career, might fix his eyes upon Francis Thompson rather than upon Sir Hall Caine; the eager young clergyman might dream dreams over the Life of Father Damien more often than over the Life of the Archbishop of Canterbury; but to what star can the eager young barrister hitch his wagon, save to the star of material success? If he does not see himself as Sir Edward Carson, it is only because he thinks that perhaps after all Sir John Simon's manner is the more effective.

There may be other answers to the questions I have asked than the answers I have given, but it is no answer to ask me how the law can be administered without barristers. I do not know; nor do I know how the roads can be swept without getting somebody to sweep them. But that would not disqualify me from saying that road-sweeping was an unattractive profession. So also I am entitled to my opinion about the Bar, which is this. That because it offers material victories only and never spiritual ones, that because there can be no standard by which its disciples are judged save the earthly standard, that because there is no place within its ranks for the altruist or the idealist—for these reasons the Bar is not one of the noble professions.

A WORD FOR AUTUMN

Last night the waiter put the celery on with the cheese, and I knew that summer was indeed dead. Other signs of autumn there may be—the reddening leaf, the chill in the early-morning air, the misty evenings—but none of these comes home to me so truly. There may be cool mornings in July; in a year of drought the leaves may change before their time; it is only with the first celery that summer is over.

I knew all along that it would not last. Even in April I was saying that winter would soon be here. Yet somehow it had begun to seem possible lately that a miracle might happen, that summer might drift on and on through the months—a final upheaval to crown a wonderful year. The celery settled that. Last night with the celery autumn came into its own.

There is a crispness about celery that is of the essence of October. It is as fresh and clean as a rainy day after a spell of heat. It crackles pleasantly in the mouth. Moreover it is excellent, I am told, for the complexion. One is always hearing of things which are good for the complexion, but there is no doubt that celery stands high on the list. After the burns and freckles of summer one is in need of something. How good that celery should be there at one's elbow.

A week ago—("A little more cheese, waiter") —a week ago I grieved for the dying summer. I wondered how I could possibly bear the waiting —the eight long months till May. In vain to comfort myself with the thought that I could get through more work in the winter undistracted by thoughts of cricket grounds and country houses. In vain, equally, to tell myself that I could stay in bed later in the mornings. Even the thought of after- breakfast pipes in front of the fire left me cold. But now, suddenly, I am reconciled to autumn. I see quite clearly that all good things must come to an end. The summer has been splendid, but it has lasted long enough. This morning I welcomed the chill in the air; this morning I viewed the falling leaves with cheerfulness; and this morning I said to myself, "Why, of course, I'll have celery for lunch." ("More bread, waiter.") "Season of mists and mellow fruitfulness," said Keats, not actually picking out celery in so many words, but plainly including it in the general blessings of the autumn. Yet what an opportunity he missed by not concentrating on that precious root. Apples, grapes, nuts, and vegetable marrows he mentions specially—and how poor a selection! For apples and grapes are not typical of any month, so ubiquitous are they, vegetable marrows are vegetables pour rire and have no place in any serious consideration of the seasons, while as for nuts, have we not a national song which asserts distinctly, "Here we go gathering nuts in May"? Season of mists and mellow celery, then let it be. A pat of butter underneath the bough, a wedge of cheese, a loaf of bread and—Thou.

How delicate are the tender shoots unfolded layer by layer. Of what, a whiteness is the last baby one of all, of what a sweetness his flavour. It is well that this should be the last rite of the meal—finis coronat opus—so that we may go straight on to the business of the pipe. Celery demands a pipe rather than a cigar, and it can be eaten better in an inn or a London tavern than in the home. Yes, and it should be eaten alone, for it is the only food which one really wants to hear oneself eat. Besides, in company one may have to consider the wants of others. Celery is not a thing to share with any man. Alone in your country inn you may call for the celery; but if you are wise you will see that no other traveller wanders into the room. Take warning from one who has learnt a lesson. One day I lunched alone at an inn, finishing with cheese and celery. Another traveller came in and lunched too. We did not speak—I was busy with my celery. From the other end of the table he reached across for the cheese. That was all right; it was the public cheese. But he also reached across for the celery—my private celery for which I owed. Foolishly—you know how one does—I had left the sweetest and crispest shoots till the last, tantalizing myself pleasantly with the thought of them. Horror! to see them snatched from me by a stranger. He realized later what he had done and apologized, but of what good is an apology in such circumstances? Yet at least the tragedy was not without its value. Now one remembers to lock the door.

Yes, I can face the winter with calm. I suppose I had forgotten what it was really like. I had been thinking of the winter as a horrid wet, dreary time fit only for professional football. Now I can see other things—crisp and sparkling days, long pleasant evenings, cheery fires. Good work shall be done this winter. Life shall be lived well. The end of the summer is not the end of the world. Here's to October—and, waiter, some more celery.

A CHRISTMAS NUMBER

The common joke against the Christmas number is that it is planned in July and made up in September. This enables it to be published in the middle of November and circulated in New Zealand by Christmas. If it were published in England at Christmas, New Zealand wouldn't get it till February. Apparently it is more important that the colonies should have it punctually than that we should.

Anyway, whenever it is made up, all journalists hate the Christmas number. But they only hate it for one reason—this being that the ordinary weekly number has to be made up at the same time. As a journalist I should like to devote the autumn exclusively to the Christmas number, and as a member of the public I should adore it when it came out. Not having been asked to produce such a number on my own I can amuse myself here by sketching out a plan for it. I follow the fine old tradition. First let us get the stories settled. Story No. 1 deals with the escaped convict. The heroine is driving back from the country- house ball, where she has had two or three proposals, when suddenly, in the most lonely part of the snow-swept moor, a figure springs out of the ditch and covers the coachman with a pistol. Alarms and confusions. "Oh, sir," says the heroine, "spare my aunt and I will give you all my jewels." The convict, for such it is, staggers back. "Lucy!" he cries. "Harold!" she gasps. The aunt says nothing, for she has swooned. At this point the story stops to explain how Harold came to be in knickerbockers. He had either been falsely accused or else he had been a solicitor. Anyhow, he had by this time more than paid for his folly, and Lucy still loved him. "Get in," she says, and drives him home. Next day he leaves for New Zealand in an ordinary lounge suit. Need I say that Lucy joins him later? No; that shall be left for your imagination. The End.

So much for the first story. The second is an "i'-faith-and-stap- me" story of the good old days. It is not seasonable, for most of the action takes place in my lord's garden amid the scent of roses; but it brings back to us the old romantic days when fighting and swearing were more picturesque than they are now, and when women loved and worked samplers. This sort of story can be read best in front of the Christmas log; it is of the past, and comes naturally into a Christmas number. I shall not describe its plot, for that is unimportant; it is the "stap me's" and the "la, sirs," which matter. But I may say that she marries him all right in the end, and he goes off happily to the wars.

We want another story. What shall this one be about? It might be about the amateur burglar, or the little child who reconciled old Sir John to his daughter's marriage, or the ghost at Enderby Grange, or the millionaire's Christmas dinner, or the accident to the Scotch express. Personally, I do not care for any of these; my vote goes for the desert-island story. Proud Lady Julia has fallen off the deck of the liner, and Ronald, refused by her that morning, dives off the hurricane deck—or the bowsprit or wherever he happens to be— and seizes her as she is sinking for the third time. It is a foggy night and their absence is unnoticed. Dawn finds them together on a little coral reef. They are in no danger, for several liners are due to pass in a day or two and Ronald's pockets are full of biscuits and chocolate, but it is awkward for Lady Julia, who had hoped that they would never meet again. So they sit on the beach back to back (drawn by Dana Gibson) and throw sarcastic remarks over their shoulders at each other. In the end he tames her proud spirit—I think by hiding the turtles' eggs from her—and the next liner but one takes the happy couple back to civilization.

But it is time we had some poetry. I propose to give you one serious poem about robins, and one double-page humorous piece, well illustrated in colours. I think the humorous verses must deal with hunting. Hunting does not lend itself to humour, for there are only two hunting jokes —the joke of the horse which came down at the brook and the joke of the Cockney who overrode hounds; but there are traditions to keep up, and the artist always loves it. So far we have not considered the artist sufficiently. Let us give him four full pages. One of pretty girls hanging up mistletoe, one of the squire and his family going to church in the snow, one of a brokendown coach with highwaymen coming over the hill, and one of the postman bringing loads and loads of parcels. You have all Christmas in those four pictures. But there is room for another page—let it be a coloured page, of half a dozen sketches, the period and the lettering very early English. "Ye Baron de Marchebankes calleth for hys varlet." "Ye varlet cometh righte hastilie—" You know the delightful kind of thing.

I confess that this is the sort of Christmas number which I love. You may say that you have seen it all before; I say that that is why I love it. The best of Christmas is that it reminds us of other Christmases; it should be the boast of Christmas numbers that they remind us of other Christmas numbers.

But though I doubt if I shall get quite what I want from any one number this year, yet there will surely be enough in all the numbers to bring Christmas very pleasantly before the eyes. In a dull November one likes to be reminded that Christmas is coming. It is perhaps as well that the demands of the colonies give us our Christmas numbers so early. At the same time it is difficult to see why New Zealand wants a Christmas number at all. As I glance above at the plan of my model paper I feel more than ever how adorable it would be—but not, oh not with the thermometer at a hundred in the shade.

NO FLOWERS BY REQUEST

If a statement is untrue, it is not the more respectable because it has been said in Latin. We owe the war, directly, no doubt, to the Kaiser, but indirectly to the Roman idiot who said, "Si vis pacem, para bellum." Having mislaid my Dictionary of Quotations I cannot give you his name, but I have my money on him as the greatest murderer in history.

Yet there have always been people who would quote this classical lie as if it were at least as authoritative as anything said in the Sermon on the Mount. It was said a long time ago, and in a strange language—that was enough for them. In the same way they will say, "De mortuis nil nisi bonum." But I warn them solemnly that it will take a good deal more than this to stop me from saying what I want to say about the recently expired month of February.

I have waited purposely until February was dead. Cynics may say that this was only wisdom, in that a damnatory notice from me might have inspired that unhappy month to an unusually brilliant run, out of sheer wilfulness. I prefer to think that it was good manners which forbade me to be disrespectful to her very face. It is bad manners to speak the truth to the living, but February is dead. De mortuis nil nisi veritas.

The truth about poor February is that she is the worst month of the year. But let us be fair to her. She has never had a chance. We cannot say to her, "Look upon this picture and on this. This you might have been; this you are." There is no "might have been" for her, no ideal February. The perfect June we can imagine for ourselves. Personally I do not mind how hot it be, but there must be plenty of strawberries. The perfect April—ah, one dare not think of the perfect April. That can only happen in the next world. Yet April may always be striving for it, though she never reach it. But the perfect February—what is it? I know not. Let us pity February, then, even while we blame her.

For February comes just when we are sick of winter, and therefore she may not be wintry. Wishing to do her best, she ventures her spring costume, crocus and primrose and daffodil days; days when the first faint perfume of mint is blown down the breezes, and one begins to wonder how the lambs are shaping. Is that the ideal February? Ah no! For we cannot be deceived. We know that spring is not here; that March is to come with its frosts and perchance its snows, a worse March for the milder February, a plunge back into the winter which poor February tried to flatter us was over.

Such a February is a murderer—an accessory to the murders of March. She lays the ground-bait for the victims. Out pop the stupid little flowers, eager to be deceived (one could forgive the annuals, but the perennials ought to know better by now), and down comes March, a roaring lion, to gobble them up.

And how much lost fruit do we not owe to February! One feels—a layman like myself feels—that it should be enough to have a strawberry-bed, a peach-tree, a fig-tree. If these are not enough, then the addition of a gardener should make the thing a certainty. Yet how often will not a gardener refer one back to February as the real culprit. The tree blossomed too early; the late frosts killed it; in the annoyance of the moment one may reproach the gardener for allowing it to blossom so prematurely, but one cannot absolve February of all blame.

It is no good, then, for February to try to be spring; no hope for her to please us by prolonging winter. What is left to her? She cannot even give us the pleasure of the hairshirt. Did April follow her, she could make the joys of that wonderful month even keener for us by the contrast, but—she is followed by March. What can one do with March? One does not wear a hair-shirt merely to enjoy the pleasure of following it by one slightly less hairy.

Well, we may agree that February is no good. "Oh, to be out of

43

England now that February's here," is what Browning should have said. One has no use for her in this country. Pope Gregory, or whoever it was that arranged the calendar, must have had influential relations in England who urged on him the need for making February the shortest month of the year. Let us be grateful to His Holiness that he was so persuaded. He was a little obstinate about Leap Year; a more imaginative pontiff would have given the extra day to April; but he was amenable enough for a man who only had his relations' word for it. Every first of March I raise my glass to Gregory. Even as a boy I used to drink one of his powders to him at about this time of the year.

February fill-dyke! Well, that's all that can be said for it.

THE UNFAIRNESS OF THINGS

The most interesting column in any paper (always excepting those which I write myself) is that entitled "The World's Press," wherein one may observe the world as it appears to a press of which one has for the most part never heard. It is in this column that I have just made the acquaintance of The Shoe Manufacturers' Monthly, the journal to which the elect turn eagerly upon each new moon. (Its one-time rival, The Footwear Fortnightly, has, I am told, quite lost its following.) The bon mot of the current number of The S.M.M. is a note to the effect that Kaffirs have a special fondness for boots which make a noise. I quote this simply as an excuse for referring to the old problem of the squeaky boots and the squeaky collar; the problem, in fact, of the unfairness of things.

The majors and clubmen who assist their country with columns of advice on clothes have often tried to explain why a collar squeaks, but have never done so to the satisfaction of any man of intelligence. They say that the collar is too large or too small, too dirty or too clean. They say that if you have your collars made for you (like a gentleman) you will be all right, but that if you buy the cheap, ready-made article, what can you expect? They say that a little soap on the outside of the shirt, or a little something on the inside of something else, that this, that, and the other will abate the nuisance. They are quite wrong.

The simple truth, and everybody knows it really, is that collars squeak for some people and not for others. A squeaky collar round the neck of a man is a comment, not upon the collar, but upon the man. That man is unlucky. Things are against him. Nature may have done all for him that she could, have given him a handsome outside and a noble inside, but the world of inanimate objects is against him.

We all know the man whom children or dogs love instinctively. It is a rare gift to be able to inspire this affection. The Fates have been kind to him. But to inspire the affection of inanimate things is something greater. The man to whom a collar or a window sash takes instinctively is a man who may truly be said to have luck on his side. Consider him for a moment. His collar never squeaks; his clothes take a delight in fitting him. At a dinner- party he walks as by instinct straight to his seat, what time you and I are dragging our partners round and round the table in search of our cards. The windows of taxicabs open to him easily. When he travels by train his luggage works its way to the front of the van and is the first to jump out at Paddington. String hastens to undo itself when he approaches; he is the only man who can make a decent impression with sealing-wax. If he is asked by the hostess in a crowded drawing-room to ring the bell, that bell comes out from behind the sofa where it hid from us and places itself in a convenient spot before his eyes. Asparagus stiffens itself at sight of him, macaroni winds itself round his fork.

You will observe that I am not describing just the ordinary lucky man. He may lose thousands on the Stock Exchange; he may be jilted; whenever he goes to the Oval to see Hobbs, Hobbs may be out first ball; he may invariably get mixed up in railway accidents. That is a kind of ill-luck which one can bear, not indeed without grumbling, but without rancour. The man who is unlucky to experience these things at least has the consolation of other people's sympathy; but the man who is the butt of inanimate things has no one's sympathy. We may be on a motor bus which overturns and nobody will say that it is our fault, but if our collar deliberately and maliciously squeaks, everybody will say that we ought to buy better collars; if our dinner cards hide from us, or the string of our parcel works itself into knots, we are called clumsy; our asparagus and macaroni give us a reputation for bad manners; our luggage gets us a name for dilatoriness.

I think we, we others, have a right to complain. However lucky we may be in other ways, if we have not this luck of inanimate things we have a right to complain. It is pleasant, I admit, to win £500 on the Stock Exchange by a stroke of sheer good fortune, but even in the blue of this there is a cloud, for the next £500 that we win by a stroke of shrewd business will certainly be put down to luck. Luck is given the credit of all our successes, but the other man is given the credit of all his luck. That is why we have a right to complain.

I do not know why things should conspire against a man. Perhaps there is some justice in it. It is possible—nay, probable—that the man whom things love is hated by animals and children—even by his fellow-men. Certainly he is hated by me. Indeed, the more I think of him, the more I see that he is not a nice man in any way. The gods have neglected him; he has no good qualities. He is a worm. No wonder, then, that this small compensation is doled out to him—the gift of getting on with inanimate things. This gives him (with the unthinking) a certain reputation for readiness and dexterity. If ever you meet a man with such a reputation, you will know what he really is.

Circumstances connected with the hour at which I rose this morning ordained that I should write this article in a dressing-gown. I shall now put on a collar. I hope it will squeak.

DAFFODILS

The confession-book, I suppose, has disappeared. It is twenty years since I have seen one. As a boy I told some inquisitive owner what was my favourite food (porridge, I fancy), my favourite hero in real life and in fiction, my favourite virtue in woman, and so forth. I was a boy, and it didn't really matter what were my likes and dislikes then, for I was bound to outgrow them. But Heaven help the journalist of those days who had to sign his name to opinions so definite! For when a writer has said in print (as I am going to say directly) that the daffodil is his favourite flower, simply because, looking round his room for inspiration, he has seen a bowl of daffodils on his table and thought it beautiful, it would be hard on him if some confession- album-owner were to expose him in the following issue as already committed on oath to the violet. Imaginative art would become impossible. Fortunately I have no commitments, and I may affirm that the daffodil is, and always has been, my favourite flower. Many people will put their money on the rose, but it is impossible that the rose can give them the pleasure which the daffodil gives them, just as it is impossible that a thousand pounds can give Rockefeller the pleasure which it gives you or me. For the daffodil comes, not only before the swallow comes— which is a matter of indifference, as nobody thinks any the worse of the swallow in consequence—but before all the many flowers of summer; it comes on the heels of a flowerless winter. Whereby it is as superior to the rose as an oasis in the Sahara is to champagne at a wedding.

Yes, a favourite flower must be a spring flower—there is no doubt about that. You have your choice, then, of the daffodil, the violet, the primrose, and the crocus. The bluebell comes too late, the cowslip is but an indifferent primrose; camelias and anemones and all the others which occur to you come into a different class. Well, then, will you choose the violet or the crocus? Or will you follow the legendary Disraeli and have primroses on your statue?

I write as one who spends most of his life in London, and for me the violet, the primrose, and the crocus are lacking in the same necessary quality—they pick badly. My favourite flower must adorn my house; to show itself off to the best advantage within doors it must have a long stalk. A crocus, least of all, is a flower to be plucked. I admit its charm as the first hint of spring that is vouchsafed to us in the parks, but I want it nearer home than that. You cannot pick a crocus and put it in water; nor can you be so cruel as to spoil the primrose and the violet by taking them from their natural setting; but the daffodil cries aloud to be picked. It is what it is waiting for.

"Long stalks, please." Who, being commanded by his lady to bring in flowers for the house, has not received this warning? And was there ever a stalk to equal the daffodil's for length and firmness and beauty? Other flowers must have foliage to set them off, but daffodils can stand by themselves in a bowl, and their green and yellow dress brings all spring into the room. A house with daffodils in it is a house lit up, whether or no the sun be shining outside. Daffodils in a green bowl—and let it snow if it will.

Wordsworth wrote a poem about daffodils. He wrote poems about most flowers. If a plant would be unique it must be one which had never inspired him to song. But he did not write about daffodils in a bowl. The daffodils which I celebrate are stationary; Wordsworth's lived on the banks of Ullswater, and fluttered and tossed their heads and danced in the breeze. He hints that in their company even he might have been jocose—a terrifying thought, which makes me happier to have mine safely indoors. When he first saw them there (so he says) he gazed and gazed and little thought what wealth the show to him had brought. Strictly speaking, it hadn't brought him in anything at the moment, but he must have known from his previous experiences with the daisy and the celandine that it was good for a certain amount.

49

A simple daffodil to him
Was so much matter for a slim
Volume at two and four.

You may say, of course, that I am in no better case, but then I have never reproached other people (as he did) for thinking of a primrose merely as a primrose.

But whether you prefer them my way or Wordsworth's—indoors or outdoors—will make no difference in this further matter to which finally I call your attention. Was there ever a more beautiful name in the world than daffodil? Say it over to yourself, and then say "agapanthus" or "chrysanthemum," or anything else you please, and tell me if the daffodils do not have it.

Pansies, lilies, kingcups, daisies, Let them live upon their praises; Long as there's a sun that sets, Primroses will have their glory; Long as there are violets They will have a place in story; But for flowers my bowls to fill, Give me just the daffodil.

As Wordsworth ought to have said.

A HOUSEHOLD BOOK

Once on a time I discovered Samuel Butler; not the other two, but the one who wrote The Way of All Flesh, the second-best novel in the English language. I say the second-best, so that, if you remind me of Tom Jones or The Mayor of Casterbridge or any other that you fancy, I can say that, of course, that one is the best. Well, I discovered him, just as Voltaire discovered Habakkuk, or your little boy discovered Shakespeare the other day, and I committed my discovery to the world in two glowing articles. Not unnaturally the world remained unmoved. It knew all about Samuel Butler.

Last week I discovered a Frenchman, Claude Tillier, who wrote in the early part of last century a book called Mon Oncle Benjamin, which may be freely translated My Uncle Benjamin. (I read it in the translation.) Eager as I am to be lyrical about it, I shall refrain. I think that I am probably safer with Tillier than with Butler, but I dare not risk it. The thought of your scorn at my previous ignorance of the world-famous Tillier, your amused contempt because I have only just succeeded in borrowing the classic upon which you were brought up, this is too much for me. Let us say no more about it. Claude Tillier—who has not heard of Claude Tillier? Mon oncle Benjamin—who has not read it, in French or (as I did) in American? Let us pass on to another book.

For I am going to speak of another discovery; of a book which should be a classic, but is not; of a book of which nobody has heard unless through me. It was published some twelve years ago, the last-published book of a well-known writer. When I tell you his name you will say, "Oh yes! I LOVE his books!" and you will mention SO-AND-SO, and its equally famous sequel SUCH-AND-SUCH. But when I ask you if you have read MY book, you will profess surprise, and say that you have never heard of it. "Is it as good as SO-AND-SO and SUCH-AND-SUCH?" you will ask, hardly believing that this could be possible. "Much better," I shall reply—and there, if these things were arranged properly, would be another ten per cent, in my pocket. But, believe me, I shall be quite content with your gratitude. Well, the writer of my book is Kenneth Grahame. You have heard of him? Good, I thought so. The books you have read are The Golden Age. and Dream Days. Am I not right? Thank you. But the book you have not read— my book—is The Wind in the Willows. Am I not right again? Ah, I was afraid so.

The reason why I knew you had not read it is the reason why I call it "my" book. For the last ten or twelve years I have been recommending it. Usually I speak about it at my first meeting with a stranger. It is my opening remark, just as yours is something futile about the weather. If I don't get it in at the beginning, I squeeze it in at the end. The stranger has got to have it some time. Should I ever find myself in the dock, and one never knows, my answer to the question whether I had anything to say would be, "Well, my lord, if I might just recommend a book to the jury before leaving." Mr. Justice Darling would probably pretend that he had read it, but he wouldn't deceive me.

For one cannot recommend a book to all the hundreds of people whom one has met in ten years without discovering whether it is well known or not. It is the amazing truth that none of those hundreds had heard of The Wind in the Willows until I told them about it. Some of them had never heard of Kenneth Grahame; well, one did not have to meet them again, and it takes all sorts to make a world. But most of them were in your position—great admirers of the author and his two earlier famous books, but ignorant thereafter. I had their promise before they left me, and waited confidently for their gratitude. No doubt they also spread the good news in their turn, and it is just possible that it reached you in this way, but it was to me, none the less, that your thanks were due. For instance, you may have noticed a couple of casual references to it, as if it were a classic known to all, in a famous novel published last year. It was I who introduced that novelist to it six months before. Indeed, I feel sometimes that it was I who wrote The Wind in the

Willows, and recommended it to Kenneth Grahame ... but perhaps I am wrong here, for I have not the pleasure of his acquaintance. Nor, as I have already lamented, am I financially interested in its sale, an explanation which suspicious strangers require from me sometimes.

I shall not describe the book, for no description would help it. But I shall just say this; that it is what I call a Household Book. By a Household Book I mean a book which everybody in the household loves and quotes continually ever afterwards; a book which is read aloud to every new guest, and is regarded as the touchstone of his worth. But it is a book which makes you feel that, though everybody in the house loves it, it is only you who really appreciate it at its true value, and that the others are scarcely worthy of it. It is obvious, you persuade yourself, that the author was thinking of you when he wrote it. "I hope this will please Jones," were his final words, as he laid down his pen.

Well, of course, you will order the book at once. But I must give you one word of warning. When you sit down to it, don't be so ridiculous as to suppose that you are sitting in judgment on my taste, still less on the genius of Kenneth Grahame. You are merely sitting in judgment on yourself. ... You may be worthy; I do not know. But it is you who are on trial.

LUNCH

Food is a subject of conversation more spiritually refreshing even than the weather, for the number of possible remarks about the weather is limited, whereas of food you can talk on and on and on. Moreover, no heat of controversy is induced by mention of the atmospheric conditions (seeing that we are all agreed as to what is a good day and what is a bad one), and where there can be no controversy there can be no intimacy in agreement. But tastes in food differ so sharply (as has been well said in Latin and, I believe, also in French) that a pronounced agreement in them is of all bonds of union the most intimate. Thus, if a man hates tapioca pudding he is a good fellow and my friend.

To each his favourite meal. But if I say that lunch is mine I do not mean that I should like lunch for breakfast, dinner, and tea; I do not mean that of the four meals (or five, counting supper) lunch is the one which I most enjoy—at which I do myself most complete justice. This is so far from being true that I frequently miss lunch altogether ... the exigencies of the journalistic profession. To-day, for instance, I shall probably miss it. No; what I mean is that lunch is the meal which in the abstract appeals to me most because of its catholicity.

We breakfast and dine at home, or at other people's homes, but we give ourselves up to London for lunch, and London has provided an amazing variety for us. We can have six courses and a bottle of champagne, with a view of the river, or one poached egg and a box of dominoes, with a view of the skylights; we can sit or we can stand, and without doubt we could, if we wished, recline in the Roman fashion; we can spend two hours or five minutes at it; we can have something different, every day of the week, or cling permanently (as I know one man to do) to a chop and chips—and what you do with the chips I have never discovered, for they combine so little of nourishment with so much of inconvenience that Nature can never have meant them for provender. Perhaps as counters. ... But I am wandering from my theme.

There is this of romance about lunch, that one can imagine great adventures with stockbrokers, actor-managers, publishers, and other demigods to have had their birth at the luncheon table. If it is a question of "bulling" margarine or "bearing" boot-polish, if the name for the new play is still unsettled, if there is some idea of an American edition—whatever the emergency, the final word on the subject is always the same, "Come and have lunch with me, and we'll talk it over"; and when the waiter has taken your hat and coat, and you have looked diffidently at the menu, and in reply to your host's question, "What will you drink?" have made the only possible reply, "Oh, anything that you're drinking" (thus showing him that you don't insist on a bottle to yourself)- -THEN you settle down to business, and the history of England is enlarged by who can say how many pages.

And not only does one inaugurate business matters at lunch, but one also renews old friendships. Who has not had said to him in the Strand, "Hallo, old fellow, I haven't seen you for ages; you must come and lunch with me one day"? And who has not answered, "Rather! I should love to," and passed on with a glow at the heart which has not died out until the next day, when the incident is forgotten? An invitation to dinner is formal, to tea unnecessary, to breakfast impossible, but there is a casualness, very friendly and pleasant, about invitations to lunch which make them complete in themselves, and in no way dependent on any lunch which may or may not follow.

Without having exhausted the subject of lunch in London (and I should like to say that it is now certain that I shall not have time to partake to-day), let us consider for a moment lunch in the country. I do not mean lunch in the open air, for it is obvious that there is no meal so heavenly as lunch thus eaten, and in a short article like this I have no time in which to dwell upon the obvious. I mean lunch at a country house. Now, the most pleasant feature of lunch at a country house is this—that you may sit next to whomsoever you please. At dinner she may be entrusted to quite the wrong man; at breakfast you are faced with the problem of being neither too early for her nor yet too late for a seat beside her; at tea people have a habit of taking your chair at the moment when a simple act of courtesy has drawn you from it in search of bread and butter; but at lunch you follow her in and there you are—fixed.

But there is a place, neither London nor the country, which brings out more than any other place all that is pleasant in lunch. It was really the recent experience of this which set me writing about lunch. Lunch in the train! It should be the "second meal"—about 1.30— because then you are really some distance from London and are hungry. The panorama flashes by outside, nearer and nearer comes the beautiful West; you cross rivers and hurry by little villages, you pass slowly and reverently through strange old towns … and, inside, the waiter leaves the potatoes next to you and slips away.

Well, it is his own risk. Here goes. … What I say is that, if a man really likes potatoes, he must be a pretty decent sort of fellow.

THE FRIEND OF MAN

When swords went out of fashion, walking-sticks, I suppose, came into fashion. The present custom has its advantages. Even in his busiest day the hero's sword must have returned at times to its scabbard, and what would he do then with nothing in his right hand? But our walking-sticks have no scabbards. We grasp them always, ready at any moment to summon a cab, to point out a view, or to dig an enemy in the stomach. Meanwhile we slash the air in defiance of the world.

My first stick was a malacca, silver at the collar and polished horn as to the handle. For weeks it looked beseechingly at me from a shop window, until a lucky birthday tip sent me in after it. We went back to school together that afternoon, and if anything can lighten the cloud which hangs over the last day of holidays, it is the glory of some such stick as mine. Of course it was too beautiful to live long; yet its death became it. I had left many a parental umbrella in the train unhonoured and unsung. My malacca was mislaid in an hotel in Norway. And even now when the blinds are drawn and we pull up our chairs closer round the wood fire, what time travellers tell to awestruck stay-at-homes tales of adventure in distant lands, even now if by a lucky chance Norway is mentioned, I tap the logs carelessly with the poker and drawl, "I suppose you didn't happen to stay at Vossvangen? I left a malacca cane there once. Rather a good one too." So that there is an impression among my friends that there is hardly a town in Europe but has had its legacy from me. And this I owe to my stick.

My last is of ebony, ivory-topped. Even though I should spend another fortnight abroad I could not take this stick with me. It is not a stick for the country; its heart is in Piccadilly. Perhaps it might thrive in Paris if it could stand the sea voyage. But no, I cannot see it crossing the Channel; in a cap I am no companion for it. Could I step on to the boat in a silk hat and then retire below—but I am always unwell below, and that would not suit its dignity. It stands now in a corner of my room crying aloud to be taken to the opera. I used to dislike men who took canes to Covent Garden, but I see now how it must have been with them. An ebony stick topped with ivory has to be humoured. Already I am considering a silk-lined cape, and it is settled that my gloves are to have black stitchings.

Such is my last stick, for it was given to me this very morning. At my first sight of it I thought that it might replace the common one which I lost in an Easter train. That was silly of me. I must have a stick of less gentle birth which is not afraid to be seen with a soft hat. It must be a stick which I can drop, or on occasion kick; one with which I can slash dandelions; one for which, when ultimately I leave it in a train, conscience does not drag me to Scotland Yard. In short, a companionable stick for a day's journey; a country stick.

The ideal country stick will never be found. It must be thick enough to stand much rough usage of a sort which I will explain presently, and yet it must be thin so that it makes a pleasant whistling sound through the air. Its handle must be curved so that it can pull down the spray of blossom of which you are in need, or pull up the luncheon basket which you want even more badly, and yet it must be straight so that you can drive an old golf ball with it. It must be unadorned, so that it shall lack ostentation, and yet it must have a band, so that when you throw stones at it you can count two if you hit the silver. You begin to see how difficult it is to achieve the perfect stick.

Well, each one of us must let go those properties which his own stick can do best without. For myself I insist on this—my stick must be good for hitting and good to hit with. A stick, we are agreed, is something to have in the hand when walking. But there are times when we sit down; and if our journey shall have taken us to the beach, our stick must at once be propped in the sand while from a suitable distance we throw stones at it. However beautiful the sea, its beauty can only be appreciated properly in this fashion. Scenery must not be taken at a gulp; we must absorb it unconsciously. With the mind gently exercised as to whether we scored a two on the band or a one just below it, and with the muscles of the arm at stretch, we are in a state ideally receptive of beauty.

And, for my other essential of a country stick, it must be possible to grasp it by the wrong end and hit a ball with it. So it must have no ferrule, and the handle must be heavy and straight. In this way was golf born; its creator roamed the fields after his picnic lunch, knocking along the cork from his bottle. At first he took seventy-nine from the gate in one field to the oak tree in the next; afterwards fifty-four. Then suddenly he saw the game. We cannot say that he was no lover of Nature. The desire to knock a ball about, to play silly games with a stick, comes upon a man most keenly when he is happy; let it be ascribed that he is happy to the streams and the hedges and the sunlight through the trees. And so let my stick have a handle heavy and straight, and let there be no ferrule on the end. Be sure that I have an old golf ball in my pocket.

In London one is not so particular. Chiefly we want a stick for leaning on when we are talking to an acquaintance suddenly met. After the initial "Hulloa!" and the discovery that we have nothing else of importance to say, the situation is distinctly eased by the remembrance of our stick. It gives us a support moral and physical, such as is supplied in a drawing-room by a cigarette. For this purpose size and shape are immaterial. Yet this much is essential— it must not be too slippery, or in our nervousness we may drop it altogether. My ebony stick with the polished ivory top—

But I have already decided that my ebony stick is out of place with the everyday hat. It stands in its corner waiting for the opera season, I must get another stick for rough work.

THE DIARY HABIT

A newspaper has been lamenting the decay of the diary-keeping habit, with the natural result that several correspondents have written to say that they have kept diaries all their lives. No doubt all these diaries now contain the entry, "Wrote to the Daily — — to deny the assertion that the diary-keeping habit is on the wane." Of such little things are diaries made.

I suppose this is the reason why diaries are so rarely kept nowadays—that nothing ever happens to anybody. A diary would be worth writing up if it could be written like this:—

MONDAY.—"Another exciting day. Shot a couple of hooligans on my way to business and was forced to give my card to the police. On arriving at the office was surprised to find the building on fire, but was just in time to rescue the confidential treaty between England and Switzerland. Had this been discovered by the public, war would infallibly have resulted. Went out to lunch and saw a runaway elephant in the Strand. Thought little of it at the time, but mentioned it to my wife in the evening. She agreed that it was worth recording."

TUESDAY.—"Letter from solicitor informing me that I have come into £1,000,000 through the will of an Australian gold-digger named Tomkins. On referring to my diary I find that I saved his life two years ago by plunging into the Serpentine. This is very gratifying. Was late at the office as I had to look in at the Palace on the way, in order to get knighted, but managed to get a good deal of work done before I was interrupted by a madman with a razor, who demanded £100. Shot him after a desperate struggle. Tea at an ABC, where I met the Duke of—. Fell into the Thames on my way home, but swam ashore without difficulty."

Alas! we cannot do this. Our diaries are very prosaic, very dull indeed. They read like this:—

Monday.—"Felt inclined to stay in bed this morning and send an excuse to the office, but was all right after a bath and breakfast. Worked till 1.30 and had lunch. Afterwards worked till five, and had my hair cut on the way home. After dinner read A Man's Passion, by Theodora Popgood. Rotten. Went to bed at eleven."

Tuesday.—"Had a letter from Jane. Did some good work in the morning, and at lunch met Henry, who asked me to play golf with him on Saturday. Told him I was playing with Peter, but said I would like a game with him on the Saturday after. However, it turned out he was playing with William then, so we couldn't fix anything up. Bought a pair of shoes on my way home, but think they will be too tight. The man says, though, that they will stretch."

Wednesday.—"Played dominoes at lunch and won fivepence."

If this sort of diary is now falling into decay, the world is not losing much. But at least it is a harmless pleasure to some to enter up their day's doings each evening, and in years to come it may just possibly be of interest to the diarist to know that it was on Monday, 27th April, that he had his hair cut. Again, if in the future any question arose as to the exact date of Henry's decease, we should find in this diary proof that anyhow he was alive as late as Tuesday, 28th April. That might, though it probably won't, be of great importance. But there is another sort of diary which can never be of any importance at all. I make no apology for giving a third selection of extracts.

Monday.—"Rose at nine and came down to find a letter from Mary. How little we know our true friends! Beneath the mask of outward affection there may lurk unknown to us the serpent's tooth of jealousy. Mary writes that she can make nothing for my stall at the bazaar as she has her own stall to provide for. Ate my breakfast mechanically, my thoughts being far away. What, after all, is life? Meditated deeply on the inner cosmos till lunch- time. Afterwards I lay down for an hour and composed my mind. I was angry this morning with Mary. Ah, how petty! Shall I never be free from the bonds of my own nature? Is the better self within me never to rise to the sublime heights of selflessness of which it is capable? Rose at four and wrote to Mary, forgiving her. This has been a wonderful day for the spirit."

Yes; I suspect that a good many diaries record adventures of the mind and soul for lack of stirring adventures to the body. If they cannot say, "Attacked by a lion in Bond Street to-day," they can at least say, "Attacked by doubt in St. Paul's Cathedral." Most people will prefer, in the absence of the lion, to say nothing, or nothing more important than "Attacked by the hairdresser with a hard brush"; but there are others who must get pen to paper somehow, and who find that only in regard to their emotions have they anything unique to say.

But, of course, there is ever within the breasts of all diarists the hope that their diaries may some day be revealed to the world. They may be discovered by some future generation, amazed at the simple doings of the twentieth century, or their publication may be demanded by the next generation, eager to know the inner life of the great man just dead. Best of all, they may be made public by the writers themselves in their autobiographies.

Yes; the diarist must always have his eye on a possible autobiography. "I remember," he will write in that great work, having forgotten all about it, "I distinctly remember"—and here he will refer to his diary—"meeting X. at lunch one Sunday and saying to him ..."

What he said will not be of much importance, but it will show you what a wonderful memory the distinguished author retains in his old age.

MIDSUMMER DAY

There is magic in the woods on Midsummer Day—so people tell me. Titania conducts her revels. Let others attend her court; for myself I will beg to be excused. I have no heart for revelling on Midsummer Day. On any other festival I will be as jocund as you please, but on the longest day of the year I am overburdened by the thought that from this moment the evenings are beginning to draw in. We are on the way to winter.

It is on Midsummer Day, or thereabouts, that the cuckoo changes his tune, knowing well that the best days are over and that in a little while it will be time for him to fly away. I should like this to be a learned article on "The Habits of the Cuckoo," and yet, if it were, I doubt if I should love him at the end of it. It is best to know only the one thing of him, that he lays his eggs in another bird's nest—a friendly idea—and beyond that to take him as we find him. And we find that his only habit which matters is the delightful one of saying "Cuckoo."

The nightingale is the bird of melancholy, the thrush sings a disturbing song of the good times to come, the blackbird whistles a fine, cool note which goes best with a February morning, and the skylark trills his way to a heaven far out of the reach of men; and what the lesser white-throat says I have never rightly understood. But the cuckoo is the bird of present joys; he keeps us company on the lawns of summer, he sings under a summer sun in a wonderful new world of blue and green. I think only happy people hear him. He is always about when one is doing pleasant things. He never sings when the sun hides behind banks of clouds, or if he does, it is softly to himself so that he may not lose the note. Then "Cuckoo!" he says aloud, and you may be sure that everything is warm and bright again.

But now he is leaving us. Where he goes I know not, but I think of him vaguely as at Mozambique, a paradise for all good birds who like their days long. If geography were properly taught at schools, I should know where Mozambique was, and what sort of people live there. But it may be that, with all these cuckoos cuckooing and swallows swallowing from July to April, the country is so full of immigrants that there is no room for a stable population. It may also be, of course, that Mozambique is not the place I am thinking of; yet it has a birdish sound.

The year is arranged badly. If Mr. Willett were alive he would do something about it. Why should the days begin to get shorter at the moment when summer is fully arrived? Why should it be possible for the vicar to say that the evenings are drawing in, when one is still having strawberries for tea? Sometimes I think that if June were called August, and April June, these things would be easier to bear. The fact that in what is now called August we should be telling each other how wonderfully hot it was for October would help us to bear the slow approach of winter. On a Midsummer Day in such a calendar one would revel gladly, and there would be no midsummer madness.

Already the oak trees have taken on an autumn look. I am told that this is due to a local irruption of caterpillars, and not to the waning of the summer, but it has a suspicious air. Probably the caterpillars knew. It seems strange now to reflect that there was a time when I liked caterpillars; when I chased them up suburban streets, and took them home to fondle them; when I knew them all by their pretty names, assisted them to become chrysalises, and watched over them in that unprotected state as if I had been their mother. Ah, how dear were my little charges to me then! But now I class them with mosquitoes and blight and harvesters, the pests of the countryside. Why, I would let them crawl up my arm in those happy days of old, and now I cannot even endure to have them dropping gently into my hair. And I should not know what to say to a chrysalis.

There are great and good people who know all about solstices and zeniths, and they can tell you just why it is that 24th June is so much hotter and longer than 24th December—why it is so in England, I should say. For I believe (and they will correct me if I am wrong) that at the equator the days and nights are always of equal length. This must make calling almost an impossibility, for if one cannot say to one's hostess, "How quickly the days are lengthening (or drawing in)," one might as well remain at home. "How stationary the days are remaining" might pass on a first visit, but the old inhabitants would not like it rubbed into them. They feel, I am sure, that however saddening a Midsummer Day may be, an unchanging year is much more intolerable. One can imagine the superiority of a resident who lived a couple of miles off the equator, and took her visitors proudly to the end of the garden where the seasons were most mutable. There would be no bearing with her.

In these circumstances I refuse to be depressed. I console myself with the thought that if 25th June is the beginning of winter, at least there is a next summer to which I may look forward. Next summer anything may happen. I suppose a scientist would be considerably surprised if the sun refused to get up one morning, or, having got up, declined to go to bed again. It would not surprise ME. The amazing thing is that Nature goes on doing the same things in the same way year after year; any sudden little irrelevance on her part would be quite understandable. When the wise men tell us so confidently that there will be an eclipse of the sun in 1921, invisible at Greenwich, do they have no qualms of doubt as the day draws near? Do they glance up from their whitebait at the appointed hour, just in case it IS visible after all? Or if they have journeyed to Pernambuco, or wherever the best view is to be obtained, do they wonder … perhaps … and tell each other the night before that, of course, they were coming to Pernambuco anyhow, to see an aunt?

Perhaps they don't. But for myself I am not so certain, and I have hopes that, certainly next year, possibly even this year, the days will go on lengthening after midsummer is over.

AT THE BOOKSTALL

I have often longed to be a grocer. To be surrounded by so many interesting things— sardines, bottled raspberries, biscuits with sugar on the top, preserved ginger, hams, brawn under glass, everything in fact that makes life worth living; at one moment to walk up a ladder in search of nutmeg, at the next to dive under a counter in pursuit of cinnamon; to serve little girls with a ha'porth of pear drops and lordly people like you and me with a pint of cherry gin —is not this to follow the king of trades? Some day I shall open a grocer's shop, and you will find me in my spare evenings aproned behind the counter. Look out for the currants in the window as you come in—I have an idea for something artistic in the way of patterns there; but, as you love me, do not offer to buy any. We grocers only put the currants out for show, and so that we may run our fingers through them luxuriously when business is slack. I have a good line in shortbreads, madam, if I can find the box, but no currants this evening, I beg you.

Yes, to be a grocer is to live well; but, after all, it is not to see life. A grocer, in as far as it is possible to a man who sells both scented soap and pilchards, would become narrow. We do not come into contact with the outside world much, save through the medium of potted lobster, and to sell a man potted lobster is not to have our fingers on his pulse. Potted lobster does not define a man. All customers are alike to the grocer, provided their money is good. I perceive now that I was over-hasty in deciding to become a grocer. That is rather for one's old age. While one is young, and interested in persons rather than in things, there is only one profession to follow—the profession of bookstall clerk.

To be behind a bookstall is indeed to see life. The fascination of it struck me suddenly as 1 stood in front of a station bookstall last Monday and wondered who bought the tie-clips. The answer came to me just as I got into my train— Ask the man behind the bookstall. He would know. Yes, and he would know who bought all his papers and books and pamphlets, and to know this is to know something about the people in the world. You cannot tell a man by the lobster he eats, but you can tell something about him by the literature he reads.

For instance, I once occupied a carriage on an eastern line with, among others, a middle-aged woman. As soon as we left Liverpool Street she produced a bag of shrimps, grasped each individual in turn firmly by the head and tail, and ate him. When she had finished, she emptied the ends out of the window, wiped her hands, and settled down comfortably to her paper. What paper? You'll never guess; I shall have to tell you—The Morning Post. Now doesn't that give you the woman? The shrimps alone, no; the paper alone, no; but the two to-gether. Conceive the holy joy of the bookstall clerk as she and her bag of shrimps— yes, he could have told at once they were shrimps—approached and asked for The Morning Post.

The day can never be dull to the bookstall clerk. I imagine him assigning in his mind the right paper to each customer. This man will ask for Golfing—wrong, he wants Cage Birds; that one over there wants The Motor—ah, well, The Auto-Car, that's near enough. Soon he would begin to know the different types; he would learn to distinguish between the patrons of The Dancing Times and of The Vote, The Era and The Athenaeum. Delightful surprises would overwhelm him at intervals; as when—a red-letter day in all the great stations—a gentleman in a check waistcoat makes the double purchase of Homer's Penny Stories and The Spectator. On those occasions, and they would be very rare, his faith in human nature would begin to ooze away, until all at once he would tell himself excitedly that the man was obviously an escaped criminal in disguise, rather overdoing the part. After which he would hand over The Winning Post and The Animals' Friend to the pursuing detective in a sort of holy awe. What a life!

But he has other things than papers to sell. He knows who buys those little sixpenny books of funny stories—a problem which has often puzzled us others; he understands by now the type of man who wants to read up a few good jokes to tell them down at old Robinson's, where he is going for the week-end. Our bookstall clerk doesn't wait to be asked. As soon as this gentleman approaches, he whips out the book, dusts it, and places it before the raconteur. He recognizes also at a glance the sort of silly ass who is always losing his indiarubber umbrella ring. Half-way across the station he can see him, and he hastens to get a new card out in readiness. ("Or we would let you have seven for sixpence, sir.") And even when one of those subtler characters draws near, about whom it is impossible to say immediately whether they require a fountain pen with case or the Life and Letters, reduced to 3s. 6d., of Major-General Clement Bulger, C.B., even then the man behind the bookstall is not found wanting. If he is wrong the first time, he never fails to recover with his second. "Bulger, sir. One of our greatest soldiers."

I thought of these things last Monday, and definitely renounced the idea of becoming a grocer; and as I wandered round the bookstall, thinking, I came across a little book, sixpence in cloth, a shilling in leather, called Proverbs and Maxims. It contained some thousands of the best thoughts in all languages, such as have guided men along the path of truth since the beginning of the world, from "What ho, she bumps!" to "Ich dien," and more. The thought occurred to me that an interesting article might be extracted from it, so I bought the book. Unfortunately enough I left it in the train before I had time to master it. I shall be at the bookstall next Monday and I shall have to buy another copy. That will be all right; you shan't miss it.

But I am wondering now what the bookstall clerk will make of me. A man who keeps on buying Proverbs and Maxims. Well, as I say, they see life.

"WHO'S WHO"

I like my novels long. When I had read three pages of this one I glanced at the end, and found to my delight that there were two thousand seven hundred and twenty-five pages more to come. I returned with a sigh of pleasure to page 4. I was just at the place where Leslie Patrick Abercrombie wins the prize "for laying out Prestatyn," some local wrestler, presumably, who had challenged the crowd at a country fair. After laying him out, Abercrombie returns to his books and becomes editor of the Town Planning Review. A wonderfully drawn character.

The plot of this oddly named novel is too complicated to describe at length. It opens with the conferment of the C.M.G. on Kuli Khan Abbas in 1903, an incident of which the anonymous author might have made a good deal more, and closes with a brief description of the Rev. Samuel Marinus Zwemer's home in New York City; but much has happened in the meanwhile. Thousands of characters have made their brief appearance on the stage, and have been hustled off to make room for others, but so unerringly are they drawn that we feel that we are in the presence of living people. Take Colette Willy, for example, who comes in on page 2656 at a time when the denouement is clearly at hand. The author, who is working up to his great scene —the appointment of Dr. Norman Wilsmore to the International Commission for the Publication of Annual Tables of Physical and Chemical Constants— draws her for us in a few lightning touches. She is "authoress, actress." She has written two little books: Dialogue de Betes and La Retraite Sentimentale. That is all. But is it not enough? Has he not made Colette Willy live before us? A lesser writer might have plunged into elaborate details about her telephone number and her permanent address, but, like the true artist that he is, our author leaves all those things unsaid. For though he can be a realist when necessary (as in the case of Wallis Budge, to which I shall refer directly), he does not hesitate to trust to the impressionist sketch when the situation demands it.

Wallis Budge is apparently the hero of the tale; at any rate, the author devotes most space to him—some hundred and twenty lines or so. He does not appear until page 341, by which time we are on familiar terms with some two or three thousand of the less important characters. It is typical of the writer that, once he has described a character to us, has (so to speak) set him on his feet, he appears to lose interest in his creation, and it is only rarely that further reference is made to him. Alfred Budd, for instance, who became British Vice-Consul of San Sebastian in 1907, and resides, as the intelligent reader will have guessed, at the San Sebastian British Vice-Consulate, obtains the M.V.O. in 1908. Nothing is said, however, of the resultant effect on his character, nor is any adequate description given—either then or later—of the San Sebastian scenery. On the other hand, Bucy, who first appears on page 340, turns up again on page 644 as the Marquess de Bucy, a Grandee of Spain. I was half-expecting that the body would be discovered about this time, but the author is still busy over his protagonists, and only leaves the Marquess in order to introduce to us his three musketeers, de Bunsen, de Burgh, and de Butts.

But it is time that I returned to our hero, Dr. Wallis Budge. Although Budge is a golfer of world-wide experience, having "conducted excavations in Egypt, the Island of Meroe, Nineveh and Mesopotamia," it is upon his mental rather than his athletic abilities that the author dwells most lovingly. The fact that in 1886 he wrote a pamphlet upon The Coptic History of Elijah the Tishbite, and followed it up in 1888 with one on The Coptic Martyrdom of George of Cappadocia (which is, of course, in every drawing-room) may not seem at first to have much bearing upon the tremendous events which followed later. But the author is artistically right in drawing our attention to them; for it is probable that, had these popular works not been written, our hero would never have been encouraged to proceed with his Magical Texts of Za-Walda-

Hawaryat, Tasfa Maryam, Sebhat-Le'ab, Gabra Shelase Tezasu, Aheta-Mikael, which had such a startling effect on the lives of all the other characters, and led indirectly to the finding of the blood-stain on the bath-mat. My own suspicions fell immediately upon Thomas Rooke, of whom we are told nothing more than "R.W.S.," which is obviously the cabbalistic sign of some secret society.

One of the author's weaknesses is a certain carelessness in the naming of his characters. For instance, no fewer than two hundred and forty-one of them are called Smith. True, he endeavours to distinguish between them by giving them such different Christian names as John, Henry, Charles, and so forth, but the result is bound to be confusing. Sometimes, indeed, he does not even bother to distinguish between their Christian names. Thus we have three Henry Smiths, who appear to have mixed themselves up even in the author's mind. He tells us that Colonel Henry's chief recreation is "the study of the things around him," but it sounds much more like that of the Reverend Henry, whose opportunities in the pulpit would be considerably greater. It is the same with the Thomsons, the Williamses and others. When once he hits upon one of these popular names, he is carried away for several pages, and insists on calling everybody Thomson. But occasionally he has an inspiration. Temistocle Zammit is a good name, though the humour of calling a famous musician Zimbalist is perhaps a little too obvious.

In conclusion, one can say that while our author's merits are many, his faults are of no great moment. Certainly he handles his love-scenes badly. Many of his characters are married but he tells us little of the early scenes of courtship, and says nothing of any previous engagements which were afterwards broken off. Also, he is apparently incapable of describing a child, unless it is the offspring of titled persons and will itself succeed to the title; even then he prefers to dismiss it in a parenthesis. But as a picture of the present-day Englishman his novel can hardly be surpassed. He is not a writer who is only at home with one class. He can describe the utterly unknown and unimportant with as much gusto as he describes the genius or the old nobility. True, he overcrowds his canvas, but one must recognize this as his method. It is so that he expresses himself best; just as one painter can express himself best in a rendering of the whole Town Council of Slappenham, while another only requires a single haddock on a plate.

His future will be watched with interest. He hints in his introduction that he has another volume in preparation, in which he will introduce to us several entirely new C.B.E.'s, besides carrying on the histories (in the familiar manner of our modern novelists) of many of those with whom we have already made friends. Who's Who, 1920, it is to be called, and I, for one, shall look out for it with the utmost eagerness.

A DAY AT LORD'S

When one has been without a certain pleasure for a number of years, one is accustomed to find on returning to it that it is not quite so delightful as one had imagined. In the years of abstinence one had built up too glowing a picture, and the reality turns out to be something much more commonplace. Pleasant, yes; but, after all, nothing out of the ordinary. Most of us have made this discovery for ourselves in the last few months of peace. We have been doing the things which we had promised ourselves so often during the war, and though they have been jolly enough, they are not quite all that we dreamed in France and Flanders. As for the negative pleasures, the pleasure of not saluting or not attending medical boards, they soon lose their first freshness.

Yet I have had one pre-war pleasure this week which carried with it no sort of disappointment. It was as good as I had thought it would be. I went to Lord's and watched first-class cricket again.

There are people who want to "brighten cricket." They remind me of a certain manager to whom I once sent a play. He told me, more politely than truthfully, how much he had enjoyed reading it, and then pointed out what was wrong with the construction. "You have two brothers here," he said. "They oughtn't to have been brothers, they should have been strangers. Then one of them marries the heroine. That's wrong; the other one ought to have married her. Then there's Aunt Jane—she strikes me as a very colourless person. If she could have been arrested in the second act for bigamy— And then I should leave out your third act altogether, and put the fourth act at Monte Carlo, and let the heroine be blackmailed by— what's the fellow's name? See what I mean?" I said that I saw. "You don't mind my criticizing your play?" he added carelessly. I said that he wasn't criticizing my play. He was writing another one—one which I hadn't the least wish to write myself.

73

And this is what the brighteners of cricket are doing. They are inventing a new game, a game which those of us who love cricket have not the least desire to watch. If anybody says that he finds Lord's or the Oval boring, I shall not be at all surprised; the only thing that would surprise me would be to hear that he found it more boring than I find Epsom or Newmarket. Cricket is not to everybody's taste; nor is racing. But those who like cricket like it for what it is, and they don't want it brightened by those who don't like it. Lord Lonsdale, I am sure, would hate me to brighten up Newmarket for him.

Lord's as it is, which is as it was five years ago, is good enough for me. I would not alter any of it. To hear the pavilion bell ring out again was to hear the most musical sound in the world. The best note is given at 11.20 in the morning; later on it lacks something of its early ecstasy. When people talk of the score of this or that opera I smile pityingly to myself. They have never heard the true music. The clink of ice against glass gives quite a good note on a suitable day, but it has not the magic of the Lord's bell.

As was my habit on these occasions five years ago, I bought a copy of The Daily Telegraph on entering the ground. In the ordinary way I do not take in this paper, but I have always had a warm admiration for it, holding it to have qualities which place it far above any other London journal of similar price. For the seats at Lord's are uncommonly hard, and a Daily Telegraph, folded twice and placed beneath one, brings something of the solace which good literature will always bring. My friends had noticed before the war, without being able to account for it, that my views became noticeably more orthodox as the summer advanced, only to fall away again with the approach of autumn. I must have been influenced subconsciously by the leading articles.

It rained, and play was stopped for an hour or two. Before the war I should have been annoyed about this, and I should have said bitterly that it was just my luck. But now I felt that I was indeed lucky thus to recapture in one day all the old sensations. It was delightful to herald again a break in the clouds, and to hear the crowd clapping hopefully as soon as ever the rain had ceased; to applaud the umpires, brave fellows, when they ventured forth at last to inspect the pitch; to realize from the sudden activity of the groundsmen that the decision was a favourable one; to see the umpires, this time in their white coats, come out again with the ball and the bails; and so to settle down once more to the business of the day.

Perhaps the cricket was slow from the point of view of the follower of league football, but I do not feel that this is any condemnation of it. An essay of Lamb's would be slow to a reader of William le Queux's works, who wanted a new body in each chapter. I shall not quarrel with anyone who holds that a day at Lord's is a dull day; if he thinks so, let him take his amusement elsewhere. But let him not quarrel with me, because I keep to my opinion, as firmly now as before the war, that a day at Lord's is a joyous day. If he will leave me the old Lord's, I will promise not to brighten his football for him.

BY THE SEA

It is very pleasant in August to recline in Fleet Street, or wherever stern business keeps one, and to think of the sea. I do not envy the millions at Margate and Blackpool, at Salcombe and Minehead, for I have persuaded myself that the sea is not what it was in my day. Then the pools were always full of starfish; crabs—really big crabs—stalked the deserted sands; and anemones waved their feelers at you from every rock.

Poets have talked of the unchanging sea (and they may be right as regards the actual water), but I fancy that the beach must be deteriorating. In the last ten years I don't suppose I have seen more than five starfishes, though I have walked often enough by the margin of the waves —and not only to look for lost golf balls. There have been occasional belated little crabs whom I have interrupted as they were scuttling home, but none of those dangerous monsters to whom in fearful excitement, and as a challenge to one's companion, one used to offer a forefinger. I refuse regretfully your explanation that it is my finger which is bigger; I should like to think that it were indeed so, and that the boys and girls of to-day find their crabs and starfishes in the size and quantity to which I was accustomed. But I am afraid we cannot hide it from ourselves that the supply is giving out. It is in fact obvious that one cannot keep on taking starfishes home and hanging them up in the hall as barometers without detriment to the coming race.

We had another amusement as children, in which I suppose the modern child is no longer able to indulge. We used to wait until the tide was just beginning to go down, and then start to climb round the foot of the cliffs from one sandy bay to another. The waves lapped the cliffs, a single false step would have plunged us into the sea, and we had all the excitement of being caught by the tide without any of the danger. We had the further excitement, if we were lucky, of seeing frantic people waving to us from the top of the cliff, people of inconceivable ignorance, who thought that the tide was coming up and that we were in desperate peril. But it was a very special day when that happened.

I have done a little serious climbing since those days, but not any which was more enjoyable. The sea was never more than a foot below us and never more than two feet deep, but the shock of falling into it would have been momentarily as great as that of falling down a precipice. You had therefore the two joys of climbing — the physical pleasure of the accomplished effort, and the glorious mental reaction when your heart returns from the middle of your throat to its normal place in your chest. And you had the additional advantages that you couldn't get killed, and that, if an insuperable difficulty presented itself, you were not driven back, but merely waited five minutes for the tide to lower itself and disclose a fresh foothold.

But, as I say, these are not joys for the modern child. The tide, I dare say, is not what it was — it does not, perhaps, go down so certainly. Or the cliffs are of a different and of an inferior shape. Or people are no longer so ignorant as to mistake the nature of your position. One way or another I expect I do better in Fleet Street. I shall stay and imagine myself by the sea; I shall not disappoint myself with the reality.

But I imagine myself away from bands and piers; for a band by a moonlit sea calls you to be very grown-up, and the beach and the crabs — such as are left — call you to be a child; and between the two you can very easily be miserable. I can see myself with a spade and bucket being extraordinarily happy. The other day I met a lucky little boy who had a pile of sand in his garden to play with, and I was fortunate enough to get an order for a tunnel. The tunnel which I constructed for him was a good one, but not so good that I couldn't see myself building a better one with practice. I came away with an ambition for architecture. If ever I go to the sea again I shall build a proper tunnel; and afterwards— well, we shall see. At the moment I feel in tremendous form. I feel that I could do a cathedral.

There is one joy of childhood, however, which one can never recapture, and that is the joy of getting wet in the sea. There is a statue not so far from Fleet Street of the man who introduced Sunday schools into England, but the man whom boys and girls would really like to commemorate in lasting stone is the doctor who first said that salt water couldn't give you a cold. Whether this was true or not I do not know, but it was a splendid and never-failing retort to anxious grown-ups, and added much to the joys of the seaside. But it is a joy no longer possible to one who is his own master. I, for instance, can get my feet wet in fresh water if I like; to get them wet in salt water is no special privilege.

Feeling as I do, writing as I have written, it is sad for me to know that if I really went to the sea this August it would not be with a spade and a bucket but with a bag of golf clubs; that even my evenings would be spent, not on the beach, but on a bicycle riding to the nearest town for a paper. Yet it is useless for you to say that I do not love the sea with my old love, that I am no longer pleased with the old childish things. I shall maintain that it is the sea which is not what it was, and that I am very happy in Fleet Street thinking of it as it used to be.

GOLDEN FRUIT

Of the fruits of the year I give my vote to the orange. In the first place it is a perennial—if not in actual fact, at least in the greengrocer's shop. On the days when dessert is a name given to a handful of chocolates and a little preserved ginger, when macêdoine de fruits is the title bestowed on two prunes and a piece of rhubarb, then the orange, however sour, comes nobly to the rescue; and on those other days of plenty when cherries and strawberries and raspberries and gooseberries riot together upon the table, the orange, sweeter than ever, is still there to hold its own. Bread and butter, beef and mutton, eggs and bacon, are not more necessary to an ordered existence than the orange.

It is well that the commonest fruit should be also the best. Of the virtues of the orange I have not room fully to speak. It has properties of health-giving, as that it cures influenza and establishes the complexion. It is clean, for whoever handles it on its way to your table but handles its outer covering, its top coat, which is left in the hall. It is round, and forms an excellent substitute with the young for a cricket ball. The pips can be flicked at your enemies, and quite a small piece of peel makes a slide for an old gentleman.

But all this would count nothing had not the orange such delightful qualities of taste. I dare not let myself go upon this subject. I am a slave to its sweetness. I grudge every marriage in that it means a fresh supply of orange blossom, the promise of so much golden fruit cut short. However, the world must go on.

Next to the orange I place the cherry. The cherry is a companionable fruit. You can eat it while you are reading or talking, and you can go on and on, absent-mindedly as it were, though you must mind not to swallow the stone. The trouble of disengaging this from the fruit is just sufficient to make the fruit taste sweeter for the labour. The stalk keeps you from soiling your fingers; it enables you also to play bob cherry. Lastly, it is by means of cherries that one penetrates the great mysteries of life—when and whom you will marry, and whether she really loves you or is taking you for your worldly prospects. (I may add here that I know a girl who can tie a knot in the stalk of a cherry with her tongue. It is a tricky business, and I am doubtful whether to add it to the virtues of the cherry or not.)

There are only two ways of eating strawberries. One is neat in the strawberry bed, and the other is mashed on the plate. The first method generally requires us to take up a bent position under a net—in a hot sun very uncomfortable, and at any time fatal to the hair. The second method takes us into the privacy of the home, for it demands a dressing-gown and no spectators. For these reasons I think the strawberry an overrated fruit. Yet I must say that I like to see one floating in cider cup. It gives a note of richness to the affair, and excuses any shortcomings in the lunch itself.

Raspberries are a good fruit gone wrong. A raspberry by itself might indeed be the best fruit of all; but it is almost impossible to find it alone. I do not refer to its attachment to the red currant; rather to the attachment to it of so many of our dumb little friends. The instinct of the lower creatures for the best is well shown in the case of the raspberry. If it is to be eaten it must be picked by the hand, well shaken, and then taken.

When you engage a gardener the first thing to do is to come to a clear understanding with him about the peaches. The best way of settling the matter is to give him the carrots and the black currants and the rhubarb for himself, to allow him a free hand with the groundsel and the walnut trees, and to insist in return for this that you should pick the peaches when and how you like. If he is a gentleman he will consent. Supposing that some satisfactory arrangement were come to, and supposing also that you had a silver-bladed pocket-knife with which you could peel them in the open air, then peaches would come very high in the list of fruits. But the conditions are difficult.

Gooseberries burst at the wrong end and smother you; melons—as the nigger boy discovered—make your ears sticky; currants, when you have removed the skin and extracted the seeds, are unsatisfying; blackberries have the faults of raspberries without their virtues; plums are never ripe. Yet all these fruits are excellent in their season. Their faults are faults which we can forgive during a slight acquaintance, which indeed seem but pleasant little idiosyncrasies in the stranger. But we could not live with them.

Yet with the orange we do live year in and year out. That speaks well for the orange. The fact is that there is an honesty about the orange which appeals to all of us. If it is going to be bad— for even the best of us are bad sometimes —it begins to be bad from the outside, not from the inside. How many a pear which presents a blooming face to the world is rotten at the core. How many an innocent-looking apple is harbouring a worm in the bud. But the orange has no secret faults. Its outside is a mirror of its inside, and if you are quick you can tell the shopman so before he slips it into the bag.

SIGNS OF CHARACTER

Wellington is said to have chosen his officers by their noses and chins. The standard for them in noses must have been rather high, to judge by the portraits of the Duke, but no doubt he made allowances. Anyhow, by this method he got the men he wanted. Some people, however, may think that he would have done better to have let the mouth be the deciding test. The lines of one's nose are more or less arranged for one at birth. A baby, born with a snub nose, would feel it hard that the decision that he would be no use to Wellington should be come to so early. And even if he arrived in the world with a Roman nose, he might smash it up in childhood, and with it his chances of military fame. This, I think you will agree with me, would be unfair.

Now the mouth is much more likely to be a true index of character. A man may clench his teeth firmly or smile disdainfully or sneer, or do a hundred things which will be reflected in his mouth rather than in his nose or chin. It is through the mouth and eyes that all emotions are expressed, and in the mouth and eyes therefore that one would expect the marks of such emotions to be left. I did read once of a man whose nose quivered with rage, but it is not usual; I never heard of anyone whose chin did anything. It would be absurd to expect it to.

But there arises now the objection that a man may conceal his mouth, and by that his character, with a moustache. There arises, too, the objection that a person whom you thought was a fool, because he always went about with his mouth open, may only have had a bad cold in the head. In fact the difficulties of telling anyone's character by his face seem more insuperable every moment. How, then, are we to tell whether we may safely trust a man with our daughter, or our favourite golf club, or whatever we hold most dear?

Fortunately a benefactor has stepped in at the right moment with an article on the cigar-manner. Our gentleman has made the discovery that you can tell a man's nature by the way he handles his cigar, and he gives a dozen illustrations to explain his theory. True, this leaves out of account the men who don't smoke cigars; although, of course, you might sum them all up, with a certain amount of justification, as foolish. But you do get, I am assured, a very important index to the characters of smokers— which is as much as to say of the people who really count.

I am not going to reveal all the clues to you now; partly because I might be infringing the copyright of another, partly because I have forgotten them. But the idea roughly is that if a man holds his cigar between his finger and thumb, he is courageous and kind to animals (or whatever it may be), and if he holds it between his first and second fingers he is impulsive but yet considerate to old ladies, and if he holds it upside down he is (besides being an ass) jealous and self-assertive, and if he sticks a knife into the stump so as to smoke it to the very end he is— yes, you have guessed this one—he is mean. You see what a useful thing a cigar may be.

I think now I am sorry that this theory has been given to the world. Yes; I blame myself for giving it further publicity. In the old days when we bought—or better, had presented to us—a cigar, a doubt as to whether it was a good one was all that troubled us. We bit one end and lit the other, and, the doubt having been solved, proceeded tranquilly to enjoy ourselves. But all this will be changed now. We shall be horribly self- conscious. When we take our cigars from our mouths we shall feel our neighbours' eyes rooted upon our hands, the while we try to remember which of all the possible manipulations is the one which represents virtue at its highest power. Speaking for myself, I hold my cigar in a dozen different ways during an evening (though never, of course, on the end of a knife), and I tremble to think of the diabolically composite nature which the modern Wellingtons of the table must attribute to me. In future I see that I must concentrate on one method. If only I could remember the one which shows me at my best!

But the tobacco test is not the only one. We may be told by the way we close our hands; the tilt of a walking-stick may unmask us. It is useless to model ourselves now on the strong, silent man of the novel whose face is a shutter to hide his emotions. This is a pity; yes, I am convinced now that it is a pity. If my secret fault is cheque-forging I do not want it to be revealed to the world by the angle of my hat; still less do I wish to discover it in a friend whom I like or whom I can beat at billiards.

How dull the world would be if we knew every acquaintance inside out as soon as we had offered him our cigar-case. Suppose—I put an extreme case to you—suppose a pleasant young bachelor who admired our bowling showed himself by his shoe laces to be a secret wife-beater. What could we do? Cut so unique a friend? Ah no. Let us pray to remain in ignorance of the faults of those we like. Let us pray it as sincerely as we pray that they shall remain in ignorance of ours.

INTELLECTUAL SNOBBERY

A good many years ago I had a painful experience. I was discovered by my house-master reading in bed at the unauthorized hour of midnight. Smith minor in the next bed (we shared a candle) was also reading. We were both discovered. But the most annoying part of the business, as it seemed to me then, was that Smith minor was discovered reading Alton Locke, and that I was discovered reading Marooned Among Cannibals. If only our house- master had come in the night before! Then he would have found me reading Alton Locke. Just for a moment it occurred to me to tell him this, but after a little reflection I decided that it would be unwise. He might have misunderstood the bearings of the revelation.

There is hardly one of us who is proof against this sort of intellectual snobbery. A detective story may have been a very good friend to us, but we don't want to drag it into the conversation; we prefer a casual reference to The Egoist, with which we have perhaps only a bowing acquaintance; a reference which leaves the impression that we are inseparable companions, or at any rate inseparable until such day when we gather from our betters that there are heights even beyond The Egoist. Dead or alive, we would sooner be found with a copy of Marcus Aurelius than with a copy of Marie Corelli. I used to know a man who carried always with him a Russian novel in the original; not because he read Russian, but because a day might come when, as the result of some accident, the "pockets of the deceased" would be exposed in the public Press. As he said, you never know; but the only accident which happened to him was to be stranded for twelve hours one August at a wayside station in the Highlands. After this he maintained that the Russians were overrated.

I should like to pretend that I myself have grown out of these snobbish ways by this time, but I am doubtful if it would be true. It happened to me not so long ago to be travelling in company of which I was very much ashamed; and to be ashamed of one's company is to be a snob. At this period I was trying to amuse myself (and, if it might be so, other people) by writing a burlesque story in the manner of an imaginary collaboration by Sir Hall Caine and Mrs. Florence Barclay. In order to do this I had to study the works of these famous authors, and for many week-ends in succession I might have been seen travelling to, or returning from, the country with a couple of their books under my arm. To keep one book beneath the arm is comparatively easy; to keep two is much more difficult. Many was the time, while waiting for my train to come in, that one of those books slipped from me. Indeed, there is hardly a junction in the railway system of the southern counties at which I have not dropped on some Saturday or other a Caine or a Barclay; to have it restored to me a moment later by a courteous fellow-passenger—courteous, but with a smile of gentle pity in his eye as he glimpsed the author's name. "Thanks very much," I would stammer, blushing guiltily, and perhaps I would babble about a sick friend to whom I was taking them, or that I was running out of paper-weights. But he never believed me. He knew that he would have said something like that himself.

Nothing is easier than to assume that other people share one's weaknesses. No doubt Jack the Ripper excused himself on the ground that it was human nature; possibly, indeed, he wrote an essay like this, in which he speculated mildly as to the reasons which made stabbing so attractive to us all. So I realize that I may be doing you an injustice in suggesting that you who read may also have your little snobberies. But I confess that I should like to cross-examine you. If in conversation with you, on the subject (let us say) of heredity, a subject to which you had devoted a good deal of study, I took it for granted that you had read Ommany's Approximations, would you make it quite clear to me that you had not read it? Or would you let me carry on the discussion on the assumption that you knew it well; would you, even, in answer to a direct question, say shamefacedly that though you had not—er—

actually read it, you—er—knew about it, of course, and had—er—read extracts from it? Somehow I think that I could lead you on to this; perhaps even make you say that you had actually ordered it from your library, before I told you the horrid truth that Ommany's Approximations was an invention of my own.

It is absurd that we (I say "we," for I include you now) should behave like this, for there is no book over which we need be ashamed, either to have read it or not to have read it. Let us, therefore, be frank. In order to remove the unfortunate impression of myself which I have given you, I will confess that I have only read three of Scott's novels, and begun, but never finished, two of Henry James'. I will also confess —and here I am by way of restoring that unfortunate impression—that I do quite well in Scottish and Jacobean circles on those five books. For, if a question arises as to which is Scott's masterpiece, it is easy for me to suggest one of my three, with the air of one who has chosen it, not over two others, but over twenty. Perhaps one of my three is the acknowledged masterpiece; I do not know. If it is, then, of course, all is well. But if it is not, then I must appear rather a clever fellow for having rejected the obvious. With regard to Henry James, my position is not quite so secure; but at least I have good reason for feeling that the two novels which I was unable to finish cannot be his best, and with a little tact I can appear to be defending this opinion hotly against some imaginary authority who has declared in favour of them. One might have read the collected works of both authors, yet make less of an impression.

Indeed, sometimes I feel that I have read their collected works, and Ommany's Approximations, and many other books with which you would be only too glad to assume familiarity. For in giving others the impression that I am on terms with these masterpieces, I have but handed on an impression which has gradually formed itself in my own mind. So I take no advantage of them; and if it appears afterwards that we have been deceived together, I shall be at least as surprised and indignant about it as they.

A QUESTION OF FORM

The latest invention on the market is the wasp gun. In theory it is something like a letter clip; you pull the trigger and the upper and lower plates snap together with a suddenness which would surprise any insect in between. The trouble will be to get him in the right place before firing. But I can see that a lot of fun can be got out of a wasp drive. We shall stand on the edge of the marmalade while the beaters go through it, and, given sufficient guns, there will not be many insects to escape. A loader to clean the weapon at regular intervals will be a necessity.

Yet I am afraid that society will look down upon the wasp gun. Anything useful and handy is always barred by the best people. I can imagine a bounder being described as "the sort of person who uses a wasp gun instead of a teaspoon." As we all know, a hat-guard is the mark of a very low fellow. I suppose the idea is that you and I, being so dashed rich, do not much mind if our straw hat does blow off into the Serpentine; it is only the poor wretch of a clerk, unable to afford a new one every day, who must take precautions against losing his first. Yet how neat, how useful, is the hat-guard. With what pride its inventor must have given birth to it. Probably he expected a statue at the corner of Cromwell Road, fitting reward for a public benefactor. He did not understand that, since his invention was useful, it was probably bad form.

Consider, again, the Richard or "dicky." Could there be anything neater or more dressy, anything more thoroughly useful? Yet you and I scorn to wear one. I remember a terrible situation in a story by Mr. W. S. Jackson. The hero found himself in a foreign hotel without his luggage. To that hotel came, with her father, the girl whom he adored silently. An invitation was given him to dinner with them, and he had to borrow what clothes he could from friendly waiters. These, alas! included a dicky. Well, the dinner began well; our hero made an excellent impression; all was gaiety. Suddenly a candle was overturned and the flame caught the heroine's frock. The hero knew what the emergency demanded. He knew how heroes always whipped off their coats and wrapped them round burning heroines. He jumped up like a bullet (or whatever jumps up quickest) and — remembered.

He had a dicky on! Without his coat, he would discover the dicky to the one person of all from whom he wished to hide it. Yet if he kept his coat on, she might die. A truly horrible dilemma. I forget which horn he impaled himself upon, but I expect you and I would have kept the secret of the Richard at all costs. And what really is wrong with a false shirt-front? Nothing except that it betrays the poverty of the wearer. Laundry bills don't worry us, bless you, who have a new straw hat every day; but how terrible if it was suspected that they did.

Our gentlemanly objection to the made-up tie seems to rest on a different foundation; I am doubtful as to the psychology of that. Of course it is a deception, but a deception is only serious when it passes itself off as something which really matters. Nobody thinks that a self-tied tie matters; nobody is really proud of being able to make a cravat out of a length of silk. I suppose it is simply the fact that a made-up tie saves time which condemns it; the safety razor was nearly condemned for a like reason. We of the leisured classes can spend hours over our toilet; by all means let us despise those who cannot.

As far as dress goes, a man only knows the things which a man mustn't do. It would be interesting if women would tell us what no real lady ever does. I have heard a woman classified contemptuously as one who does her hair up with two hair-pins, and no doubt bad feminine form can be observed in other shocking directions. But again it seems to be that the semblance of poverty, whether of means or of leisure, is the one thing which must be avoided.

Why, then, should the wasp gun be considered bad form? I don't know, but I have an instinctive feeling that it will be. Perhaps a wasp gun indicates a lack of silver spoons suitable for lethal uses. Perhaps it shows too careful a consideration of the marmalade. A man of money drowns his wasp in the jar with his spoon, and carelessly calls for another pot to be opened. The poor man waits on the outskirts with his gun, and the marmalade, void of corpses, can still be passed round. Your gun proclaims your poverty; then let it be avoided.

All the same I think I shall have one. I have kept clear of hat- guards and Richards and made-up ties without quite knowing why, but honestly I have not felt the loss of them. The wasp gun is different; having seen it, I feel that I should be miserable without it. It is going to be excellent sport, wasp-shooting; a steady hand, a good eye, and a certain amount of courage will be called for. When the season opens I shall be there, good form or bad form. We shall shoot the apple-quince coverts first. "Hornet over!"

A SLICE OF FICTION

This is a jolly world, and delightful things go on in it. For instance, I had a picture post card only yesterday from William Benson, who is staying at Ilfracombe. He wrote to say that he had gone down to Ilfracombe for a short holiday, and had been much struck by the beauty of the place. On one of his walks he happened to notice that there was to be a sale of several plots of land occupying a quite unique position in front of the sea. He had immediately thought of me in connection with it. My readiness to consider a good investment had long been known to him, and in addition he had heard rumours that I might be coming down to Ilfracombe in order to recruit my health. If so, here was a chance which should be brought to my knowledge. Further particulars ... and so on. Which was extremely friendly of William Benson. In fact, my only complaint of William is that he has his letters lithographed—a nasty habit in a friend. But I have allowed myself to be carried away. It was not really of Mr. Benson that I was thinking when I said that delightful things go on in this world, but of a certain pair of lovers, the tragedy of whose story has been revealed to me in a two-line "agony" in a morning paper. When anything particularly attractive happens in real life, we express our appreciation by saying that it is the sort of thing which one reads about in books —perhaps the highest compliment we can pay to Nature. Well, the story underlying this advertisement reeks of the feuilleton and the stage.

"PAT, I was alone when you called. You heard me talking to the dog. PLEASE make appointment. —DAISY."

You will agree with me when you read this that it is almost too good to be true. There is a freshness and a naïveté about it which is only to be found in American melodrama. Let us reconstruct the situation, and we shall see at once how delightfully true to fiction real life can be.

Pat was in love with Daisy—engaged to her we may say with confidence (for a reason which will appear in a moment). But even though she had plighted her troth to him, he was jealous, miserably jealous, of every male being who approached her. One day last week he called on her at the house in Netting Hill. The parlour-maid opened the door and smiled brightly at him. "Miss Daisy is upstairs in the drawing-room," she said. "Thank you," he replied, "I will announce myself." (Now you see how we know that they were engaged. He must have announced himself in order to have reached the situation implied in the "agony," and he would not have been allowed to do so if he had not had the standing of a fiance.)

For a moment before knocking Patrick stood outside the drawing-room door, and in that moment the tragedy occurred; he heard his lady's voice. "DARLING!" it said, "she SHALL kiss her sweetest, ownest, little pupsy-wupsy."

Patrick's brow grew black. His strong jaw clenched (just like the jaws of those people on the stage), and he staggered back from the door. "This is the end," he muttered. Then he strode down the stairs and out into the stifling streets. And up in the drawing- room of the house in Netting Hill Daisy and the toy pom sat and wondered why their lord and master was so late.

Now we come to the letter which Patrick wrote to Daisy, telling her that it was all over. He would explain to her how he had "accidentally"(he would dwell upon that) accidentally overheard her and her— —(probably he was rather coarse here) exchanging terms of endearment; he would accuse her of betraying one whose only fault was that he loved her not wisely but too well; he would announce gloomily that he had lost his faith in women. All this is certain. But it would appear also that he made some such threat as this—most likely in a postscript: "It is no good your writing. There can be no explanation. Your letters will be destroyed unopened." It is a question, however, if even this would have prevented Daisy from trying an appeal by post, for though one may talk about

92

destroying letters unopened, it is an extremely difficult thing to do. I feel, therefore, that Patrick's letter almost certainly contained a P.P.S. also—to this effect: "I cannot remain in London where we have spent so many happy hours together. I am probably leaving for the Rocky Mountains to-night. Letters will not be forwarded. Do not attempt to follow me."

And so Daisy was left with only the one means of communication and explanation—the agony columns of the morning newspapers. "I was alone when you called. You heard me talking to the dog. PLEASE make appointment." In the last sentence there is just a hint of irony which I find very attractive. It seems to me to say, "Don't for heaven's sake come rushing back to Notting Hill (all love and remorse) without warning, or you might hear me talking to the cat or the canary. Make an appointment, and I'll take care that there's NOTHING in the room when you come." We may tell ourselves, I think, that Daisy understands her Patrick. In fact, I am beginning to understand Patrick myself, and I see now that the real reason why Daisy chose the agony column as the medium of communication was that she knew Patrick would prefer it. Patrick is distinctly the sort of man who likes agony columns. I am sure it was the first thing he turned to on Wednesday morning.

It occurs to me to wonder if the honeymoon will be spent at Ilfracombe. Patrick must have received William Benson's picture post card too. We have all had one. Just fancy if he HAD gone to the Rocky Mountains; almost certainly Mr. Benson's letters would not have been forwarded.

THE LABEL

On those rare occasions when I put on my best clothes and venture into society, I am always astonished at the number of people in it whom I do not know. I have stood in a crowded ball-room, or sat in a crowded restaurant, and reflected that, of all the hundreds of souls present, there was not one of whose existence I had previously had any suspicion. Yet they all live tremendously important lives, lives not only important to themselves but to numbers of friends and relations; every day they cross some sort of Rubicon; and to each one of them there comes a time when the whole of the rest of the world (including — confound it! — me) seems absolutely of no account whatever. That I had lived all these years in contented ignorance of their existence makes me a little ashamed.

To-day in my oldest clothes I have wandered through the index of The Times Literary Supplement, and I am now feeling a little ashamed of my ignorance of so many books. Of novels alone there seem to be about 900. To write even a thoroughly futile novel is, to my thinking, a work of extraordinary endurance; yet in, say, 600 houses this work has been going on, and I (and you, and all of us) have remained utterly unmoved. Well, I have been making up for my indifference this morning. I have been reading the titles of the books. That is not so good (or bad) as reading the books themselves, but it enables me to say that I have heard of such and such a novel, and in some cases it does give me a slight clue to what goes on inside.

I should imagine that the best part of writing a novel was the choosing a title. My idea of a title is that it should be something which reflects the spirit of your work and gives the hesitating purchaser some indication of what he is asked to buy. To call your book Ethnan Frame or Esther Grant or John Temple or John Merridew (I quote from the index) is to help the reader not at all.

94

All it tells him is that one of the characters inside will be called John or Esther—a matter, probably, of indifference to him. Phyllis is a better title, because it does give a suggestion of the nature of the book. No novel with a tragic ending, no powerful realistic novel, would be called Phyllis. Without having read Phyllis I should say that it was a charming story of suburban life, told mostly in dialogue, and that Phyllis herself was a perfect dear—though a little cruel about that first box of chocolates he sent her. However, she married him in the end all right.

But if you don't call your book Phyllis or John Temple or Mrs. Elmsley, what—I hear you asking—are you to call it? Well, you might call it Kapak, as I see somebody has done. The beauty of Kapak as a title is that if you come into the shop by the back entrance, and so approach the book from the wrong end, it is still Kapak. A title which looks the same from either end is of immense advantage to an author. Besides, in this particular case there is a mystery about Kapak which one is burning to solve. Is it the bride's pet name for her father-in-law, the password into the magic castle, or that new stuff with which you polish brown boots? Or is it only a camera? Let us buy the book at once and find out.

Another mystery title is The Man with Thicker Beard, which probably means something. It is like Kapak in this, that it reads equally well backwards; but it is not so subtle. Still, we should probably be lured on to buy it. On the other hand, A Welsh Nightingale and a Would-be Suffragette is just the sort of book to which we would not be tempted by the title. It is bad enough to have to say to the shopman, "Have you A Welsh Nightingale and a Would-be Suffragette?" but if we forgot the title, as we probably should, and had to ask at random for a would-be nightingale and a Welsh suffragette, or a wood nightingale and a Welsh rabbit, or the Welsh suffragette's night in gaol, we should soon begin to wish that we had decided on some quite simple book such as Greed, Earth, or Jonah.

And this is why a French title is always such a mistake. Authors must remember that their readers have not only to order the book, in many cases, verbally, but also to recommend it to their friends. So I think Mr. Oliver Onions made a mistake when he called his collection of short stories Pot au Feu. It is a good title, but it is the sort of title to which the person to whom you are recommending the book always answers, "What?" And when people say "What?" in reply to your best Parisian accent, the only thing possible for you is to change the subject altogether. But it is quite time that we came to some sort of decision as to what makes the perfect title. Kapak will attract buyers, as I have said, though to some it may not seem quite fair. Excellent from a commercial point of view, it does not satisfy the conditions we laid down at first. The title, we agreed, must reflect the spirit of the book. In one sense Five Gallons of Gasolene does this, but of course nobody could ask for that in a book-shop.

Well, then, here is a perfect title, Their High Adventure. That explains itself just sufficiently. When a Man's Married, For Henri and Navarre, and The King Over the Water are a little more obvious, but they are still good. The Love Story of a Mormon makes no attempt to deceive the purchaser, but it can hardly be called a beautiful title. Melody in Silver, on the other hand, is beautiful, but for this reason makes one afraid to buy it, lest there should be disappointment within. In fact, as I look down the index, I am beginning to feel glad that there are so many hundreds of novels which I haven't read. In most of them there would be disappointment. And really one only reads books nowadays so as to be able to say to one's neighbour on one's rare appearances in society, "HAVE you read The Forged Coupon, and WHAT do you think of The Muck Rake?" And for this an index is quite enough.

THE PROFESSION

I have been reading a little book called How to Write for the Press. Other books which have been published upon the same subject are How to Be an Author, How to Write a Play, How to Succeed as a Journalist, How to Write for the Magazines, and How to Earn £600 a Year with the Pen. Of these the last-named has, I think, the most pleasing title. Anybody can write a play; the trouble is to get it produced. Almost anybody can be an author; the business is to collect money and fame from this state of being. Writing for the magazines, again, sounds a delightful occupation, but literally it means nothing without the co- operation of the editors of the magazines, and it is this co- operation which is so difficult to secure. But to earn £600 a year with the pen is to do a definite thing; if the book could really tell the secret of that, it would have an enormous sale. I have not read it, so I cannot say what the secret is. Perhaps it was only a handbook on forgery.

How to Write for the Press disappointed me. It is concerned not with the literary journalist (as I believe he is called) but with the reporter (as he is never called, the proper title being "special representative"). It gives in tabular form a list of the facts you should ascertain at the different functions you attend; with this book in your pocket there would be no excuse if you neglected to find out at a wedding the names of the bride and bridegroom. It also gives—and I think this is very friendly of it—a list of useful synonyms for the principal subjects, animate and inanimate, of description. The danger of calling the protagonists at the court of Hymen (this one is not from the book; I thought of it myself just now)—the danger of calling them "the happy pair" more than once in a column is that your readers begin to suspect that you are a person of extremely limited mind, and when once they get this idea into their heads they are not in a proper state to appreciate the rest

97

of your article. But if in your second paragraph you speak of "the joyful couple," and in your third of "the ecstatic brace," you give an impression of careless mystery of the language which can never be shed away.

Among the many interesting chapters is one dealing with contested elections. One of the questions to which the special representative was advised to find an answer was this: "What outside bodies are taking active part in the contest?" In the bad old days—now happily gone for ever—the outside bodies of dead cats used to take an active and important part in the contest, and as the same body would often be used twice the reporter in search of statistics was placed in a position of great responsibility. Nowadays, I suppose, he is only meant to concern himself with such bodies as the Coal Consumers' League and the Tariff Reform League, and there would be no doubt in the mind of anybody as to whether they were there or not.

I am afraid I should not be a success as "our special representative." I should never think of half the things which occur to the good reporter. You read in your local paper a sentence like this: "The bride's brother, who only arrived last week from Australia, where he held an important post under the Government, and is about to proceed on a tour through Canada with—curiously enough—a nephew of the bride-groom, gave her away." Well, what a mass of information has to be gleaned before that sentence can be written. Or this. "The hall was packed to suffocation, and beneath the glare of the electric light— specially installed for this occasion by Messrs. Ampère & Son of Pumpton, the building being at ordinary times strikingly deficient in the matter of artificial lighting in spite of the efforts of the more progressive members of the town council—the faces of not a few of the fairer sex could be observed." You know, I am afraid I should have forgotten all that. I should simply have obtained a copy of the principal speech, and prefaced it with the words," Mr. Dodberry then spoke as follows"; or, if my conscience would not allow of such a palpable misstatement, "Mr. Dodberry then rose with the intention of speaking as follows."

98

In the more human art of interviewing I should be equally at fault. The interview itself would be satisfactory, but I am afraid that its publication would lead people to believe that all the best things had been said by me. To remember what anybody else has said is easy; to remember, even five minutes after, what one has said oneself is almost impossible. For to recall YOUR remarks in our argument at the club last night is simply a matter of memory; to recall MINE, I have to forget all that I meant to have said, all that I ought to have said, and all that I have thought upon the subject since.

In fact, I begin to see that the successful reporter must eliminate his personality altogether, whereas the successful literary journalist depends for his success entirely upon his personality —which is what is meant by "style." I suppose it is for this reason that, when the literary journalist is sent as "our extra-special representative" to report a prize fight or a final cup tie or a political meeting, the result is always appalling. The "ego" bulges out of every line, obviously conscious that it is showing us no ordinary reporting, determined that it will not be overshadowed by the importance of the subject. And those who are more interested in the matter than in the manner regard him as an intruder, and the others regret that he is so greatly overtaxing his strength.

So each to his business, and his handbook to each—How to Write for the Press to the special representative, and How to Be an Author to the author. There is no book, I believe, called How to Be a Solicitor, or a doctor or an admiral or a brewer. That is a different matter altogether; but any fool can write for the papers.

SMOKING AS A FINE ART

My first introduction to Lady Nicotine was at the innocent age of eight, when, finding a small piece of somebody else's tobacco lying unclaimed on the ground, I decided to experiment with it. Numerous desert island stories had told me that the pangs of hunger could be allayed by chewing tobacco; it was thus that the hero staved off death before discovering the bread-fruit tree. Every right-minded boy of eight hopes to be shipwrecked one day, and it was proper that I should find out for myself whether my authorities could be trusted in this matter. So I chewed tobacco. In the sense that I certainly did not desire food for some time afterwards, my experience justified the authorities, but I felt at the time that it was not so much for staving off death as for reconciling oneself to it that tobacco-chewing was to be recommended. I have never practised it since.

At eighteen I went to Cambridge, and bought two pipes in a case. In those days Greek was compulsory, but not more so than two pipes in a case. One of the pipes had an amber stem and the other a vulcanite stem, and both of them had silver belts. That also was compulsory. Having bought them, one was free to smoke cigarettes. However, at the end of my first year I got to work seriously on a shilling briar, and I have smoked that, or something like it, ever since.

In the last four years there has grown up a new school of pipe-smokers, by which (I suspect) I am hardly regarded as a pipe-smoker at all. This school buys its pipes always at one particular shop; its pupils would as soon think of smoking a pipe without the white spot as of smoking brown paper. So far are they from smoking brown paper that each one of them has his tobacco specially blended according to the colour of his hair, his taste in revues, and the locality in which he lives. The first blend is naturally not the ideal one. It is only when he has been a confirmed smoker for at least three months, and knows the best and worst of all tobaccos, that his exact requirements can be satisfied.

However, it is the pipe rather than the tobacco which marks him as belonging to this particular school. He pins his faith, not so much to its labour-saving devices as to the white spot outside, the white spot of an otherwise aimless life. This tells the world that it is one of THE pipes. Never was an announcement more superfluous. From the moment, shortly after breakfast, when he strikes his first match to the moment, just before bed-time, when he strikes his hundredth, it is obviously THE pipe which he is smoking.

For whereas men of an older school, like myself, smoke for the pleasure of smoking, men of this school smoke for the pleasure of pipe-owning — of selecting which of their many white-spotted pipes they will fill with their specially-blended tobacco, of filling the one so chosen, of lighting it, of taking it from the mouth to gaze lovingly at the white spot and thus letting it go out, of lighting it again and letting it go out again, of polishing it up with their own special polisher and putting it to bed, and then the pleasure of beginning all over again with another white- spotted one. They are not so much pipe-smokers as pipe-keepers; and to have spoken as I did just now of their owning pipes was wrong, for it is they who are in bondage to the white spot. This school is founded firmly on four years of war. When at the age of eighteen you are suddenly given a cheque-book and called "Sir," you must do something by way of acknowledgment. A pipe in the mouth makes it clear that there has been no mistake — you are undoubtedly a man. But you may be excused for feeling after the first pipe that the joys of smoking have been rated too high, and for trying to extract your pleasure from the polish on the pipe's surface, the pride of possessing a special mixture of your own, and such-like matters, rather than from the actual inspiration and expiration of smoke. In the same way a man not fond of reading may find delight in a library of well-bound books. They are pleasant to handle, pleasant to talk about, pleasant to show to friends. But it is the man without the library of well-bound books who generally does most of the reading.

So I feel that it is we of the older school who do most of the smoking. We smoke unconsciously while we are doing other things; THEY try, but not very successfully, to do other things while they are consciously smoking. No doubt they despise us, and tell themselves that we are not real smokers, but I fancy that they feel a little uneasy sometimes. For my young friends are always trying to persuade me to join their school, to become one of the white-spotted ones. I have no desire to be of their company, but I am prepared to make a suggestion to the founder of the school. It is that he should invent a pipe, white spot and all, which smokes itself. His pupils could hang it in the mouth as picturesquely as before, but the incidental bother of keeping it alight would no longer trouble them.

THE PATH TO GLORY

My friend Mr. Sidney Mandragon is getting on. He is now one of the great ones of the earth. He has just been referred to as "Among those present was Mr. Sidney Mandragon."

As everybody knows (or will know when they have read this article) the four stages along the road to literary fame are marked by the four different manners in which the traveller's presence at a public function is recorded in the Press. At the first stage the reporter glances at the list of guests, and says to himself, "Mr. George Meredith —never heard of him," and for all the world knows next morning, Mr. George Meredith might just as well have stayed at home. At the second stage (some years later) the reporter murmurs to his neighbour in a puzzled sort of way: "George Meredith? George Meredith? Now where have I come across that name lately? Wasn't he the man who pushed a wheelbarrow across America? Or was he the chap who gave evidence in that murder trial last week?" And, feeling that in either case his readers will be interested in the fellow, he says: "The guests included ... Mr. George Meredith and many others." At the third stage the reporter knows at last who Mr. George Meredith is. Having seen an advertisement of one of his books, and being pretty sure that the public has read none of them, he refers to him as "Mr. George Meredith, the well-known novelist." The fourth and final stage, beyond the reach of all but the favoured few, is arrived at when the reporter can leave the name to his public unticketed, and says again, "Among those present was Mr. George Meredith."

The third stage is easy to reach—indeed, too easy. The "well-known actresses" are not Ellen Terry, Irene Vanbrugh and Marie Tempest, but Miss Birdie Vavasour, who has discovered a new way of darkening the hair, and Miss Girlie de Tracy, who has been arrested for shop-lifting. In the same way, the more the Press insists that a writer is "well-known," the less hope will he have that the public has heard of him. Better far to remain at the second stage, and to flatter oneself that one has really arrived at the fourth.

But my friend Sidney Mandragon is, indeed, at the final stage now, for he had been "the well-known writer" for at least a dozen years previously. Of course, he has been helped by his name. Shakespeare may say what he likes, but a good name goes a long way in the writing profession. It was my business at one time to consider contributions for a certain paper, and there was one particular contributor whose work I approached with an awe begotten solely of his name. It was not exactly Milton, and not exactly Carlyle, and not exactly Charles Lamb, but it was a sort of mixture of all three and of many other famous names thrown in, so that, without having seen any of his work printed elsewhere, I felt that I could not take the risk of refusing it myself. "This is a good man," I would say before beginning his article; "this man obviously has style. And I shouldn't be surprised to hear that he was an authority on fishing." I wish I could remember his name now, and then you would see for yourself.

Well, take Mr. Hugh Walpole (if he will allow me). It is safe to say that, when Mr. Walpole's first book came out, the average reader felt vaguely that she had heard of him before. She hadn't actually read his famous Letters, but she had often wanted to, and—or was that his uncle? Anyway, she had often heard people talking about him. What a very talented family it was! In the same way Sidney Mandragon has had the great assistance of one of the two Christian names which carry weight in journalism. The other, of course, is Harold. If you are Sidney or Harold, the literary world is before you.

Another hall-mark by which we can tell whether a man has arrived or not is provided by the interview. If (say) a Lepidopterist is just beginning his career, nobody bothers about his opinions on anything. If he is moderately well-known in his profession, the papers will seek his help whenever his own particular subject comes up in the day's news. There is a suggestion, perhaps, in Parliament that butterflies should be muzzled, and "Our Representative" promptly calls upon "the well-known Lepidopterist" to ask what HE thinks about it. But if he be of an established reputation, then his professional opinion is no longer sought. What the world is eager for now is to be told his views on Sunday Games, the Decadence of the Theatre or Bands in the Parks.

The modern advertising provides a new scale of values. No doubt Mr. Pelman offers his celebrated hundred guineas' fee equally to all his victims, but we may be pretty sure that in his business- like brain he has each one of them nicely labelled, a Gallant Soldier being good for so much new business, a titled Man of Letters being good for slightly less; and that real Fame is best measured by the number of times that one's unbiased views on Pelmanism (or Tonics or Hair-Restorers) are considered to be worth reprinting. In this matter my friend Mandragon is doing nicely. For a suitable fee he is prepared to attribute his success to anything in reason, and his confession of faith can count upon a place in every full-page advertisement of the mixture, and frequently in the odd half-columns. I never quite understand why a tonic which has tightened up Mandragon's fibres, or a Mind-Training System which has brought General Blank's intellect to its present pitch, should be accepted more greedily by the man-in-the-street than a remedy which has only proved its value in the case of his undistinguished neighbour, but then I can never understand quite a number of things. However, that doesn't matter. All that matters at the moment is that Mr. Sidney Mandragon has now achieved glory. Probably the papers have already pigeon-holed his obituary notice. It is a pleasing thought.

A PROBLEM IN ETHICS

Life is full of little problems, which arise suddenly and find one wholly unprepared with a solution. For instance, you travel down to Wimbledon on the District Railway—first-class, let us suppose, because it is your birthday. On your arrival you find that you have lost your ticket. Now, doubtless there is some sort of recognized business to be gone through which relieves you of the necessity of paying again. You produce an affidavit of a terribly affirmative nature, together with your card and a testimonial from a beneficed member of the Church of England. Or you conduct a genial correspondence with the traffic manager which spreads itself over six months. To save yourself this bother you simply tell the collector that you haven't a ticket and have come from Charing Cross. Is it necessary to add "first- class"?

Of course one has a strong feeling that one ought to, but I think a still stronger feeling that one isn't defrauding the railway company if one doesn't. (I will try not to get so many "ones" into my next sentence.) For you may argue fairly that you established your right to travel first-class when you stepped into the carriage with your ticket—and, it may be, had it examined therein by an inspector. All that you want to do now is to establish your right to leave the Wimbledon platform for the purer air of the common. And you can do this perfectly easily with a third-class ticket.

However, this is a problem which will only arise if you are careless with your property. But however careful you are, it may happen to you at any moment that you become suddenly the owner of a shilling with a hole in it.

I am such an owner. I entered into possession a week ago—Heaven knows who played the thing off on me. As soon as I made the discovery I went into a tobacconist's and bought a box of matches.

"This," he said, looking at me reproachfully, "is a shilling with a hole in it."

"I know," I said, "but it's all right, thanks. I don't want to wear it any longer. The fact is, Joanna has thrown me—However, I needn't go into that." He passed it back to me.

"I am afraid I can't take it," he said.

"Why not? I managed to."

However, I had to give him one without a hole before he would let me out of his shop. Next time I was more thoughtful. I handed three to the cashier at my restaurant in payment of lunch, and the ventilated one was in the middle. He saw the joke of it just as I was escaping down the stairs.

"Hi!" he said, "this shilling has a hole in it."

I went back and looked at it. Sure enough it had.

"Well, that's funny," I said. "Did you drop it, or what?"

He handed the keepsake back to me. He also had something of reproach in his eye.

"Thanks, very much," I said. "I wouldn't have lost it for worlds;

Emily—But I mustn't bore you with the story. Good day to you."

And I gave him a more solid coin and went.

Well, that's how we are at present. A more unscrupulous person than myself would have palmed it off long ago. He would have told himself with hateful casuistry that the coin was none the worse for the air-hole in it, and that, if everybody who came into possession of it pressed it on to the next man, nobody would be injured by its circulation. But I cannot argue like this. It pleases me to give my shilling a run with the others sometimes. I like to put it down on a counter with one or two more, preferably in the middle of them where the draught cannot blow through it; but I should indeed be surprised—I mean sorry—if it did not come back to me at once.

There is one thing, anyhow, that I will not do. I will not give it to a waiter or a taxi-driver or to anybody else as a tip. If you estimate the market value of a shilling with a hole in it at anything from ninepence to fourpence according to the owner's chances of getting rid of it, then it might be considered possibly a handsome, anyhow an adequate, tip for a driver; but somehow the idea does not appeal to me at all. For if the recipient did not see the hole, you would feel that you had been unnecessarily generous to him, and that one last effort to have got it off on to a shopkeeper would have been wiser; while if he did see it—well, we know what cabmen are. He couldn't legally object, it is a voluntary gift on your part, and even regarded as a contribution to his watch chain worthy of thanks, but—Well, I don't like it. I don't think it's sportsmanlike.

However, I have an idea at last. I know a small boy who owns some lead soldiers. I propose to borrow one of these—a corporal or perhaps a serjeant—and boil him down, and then fill up the hole in the shilling with lead. Shillings, you know, are not solid silver; oh no, they have alloy in them. This one will have a little more than usual perhaps. One cannot tie oneself down to an ounce or two.

We set out, I believe, to discuss the morals of the question. It is a most interesting subject.

THE HAPPIEST HALF-HOURS OF LIFE

Yesterday I should have gone back to school, had I been a hundred years younger. My most frequent dream nowadays—or nowanights I suppose I should say—is that I am back at school, and trying to construe difficult passages from Greek authors unknown to me. That they are unknown is my own fault, as will be pointed out to me sternly in a moment. Meanwhile I stand up and gaze blankly at the text, wondering how it is that I can have forgotten to prepare it. "Er—him the—er—him the—the er many-wiled Odysseus—h'r'm— then, him addressing, the many-wiled Odysseus— er—addressed. Er—er —the er—" And then, sweet relief, I wake up. That is one of my dreams; and another is that I am trying to collect my books for the next school and that an algebra, or whatever you like, is missing. The bell has rung, as it seems hours ago, I am searching my shelves desperately, I am diving under my table, behind the chair ... I shall be late, I shall be late, late, late ...

No doubt I had these bad moments in real life a hundred years ago. Indeed I must have had them pretty often that they should come back to me so regularly now. But it is curious that I should never dream that I am going back to school, for the misery of going back must have left a deeper mark on my mind than all the little accidental troubles of life when there. I was very happy at school; but oh! the utter wretchedness of the last day of the holidays.

One began to be apprehensive on the Monday. Foolish visitors would say sometimes on the Monday, "When are you going back to school?" and make one long to kick them for their tactlessness. As well might they have said to a condemned criminal, "When are you going to be hanged?" or, "What kind of—er—knot do you think they'll use?" Throughout Monday and Tuesday we played the usual games, amused ourselves in the usual way, but with heavy hearts. In the excitement of the moment we would forget and be happy, and then suddenly would come the thought, "We're going back on Wednesday."

And on Tuesday evening we would bring a moment's comfort to ourselves by imagining that we were not going back on the morrow. Our favourite dream was that the school was burnt down early on Wednesday morning, and that a telegram arrived at breakfast apologizing for the occurrence, and pointing out that it would be several months before even temporary accommodation could be erected. No Vandal destroyed historic buildings so light-heartedly as we. And on Tuesday night we prayed that, if the lightnings of Heaven failed us, at least a pestilence should be sent in aid. Somehow, SOMEHOW, let the school be uninhabitable!

But the telegram never came. We woke on Wednesday morning as wakes the murderer on his last day. We took a dog or two for a walk; we pretended to play a game of croquet. After lunch we donned the badges of our servitude. The comfortable, careless, dirty flannels were taken off, and the black coats and stiff white collars put on. At 3.30 an early tea was ready for us— something rather special, a last mockery of holiday. (Dressed crab, I remember, on one occasion, and I travelled with my back to the engine after it—a position I have never dared to assume since.) Then good-byes, tips, kisses, a last look, and—the 4.10 was puffing out of the station. And nothing, nothing had happened. I can remember thinking in the train how unfair it all was. Fifty-two weeks in the year, I said to myself, and only fifteen of them spent at home. A child snatched from his mother at nine, and never again given back to her for more than two months at a time. "Is this Russia?" I said; and, getting no answer, could only comfort myself with the thought, "This day twelve weeks!"

And once the incredible did happen. It was through no intervention of Providence; no, it was entirely our own doing. We got near some measles, and for a fortnight we were kept in quarantine. I can say truthfully that we never spent a duller two weeks. There seemed to be nothing to do at all. The idea that we were working had to be fostered by our remaining shut up in one room most of the day, and within the limits of that room we found very little in the way of amusement. We were bored extremely. And always we carried with us the thought of Smith or Robinson taking our place in the Junior House team and making hundreds of runs. ...

Because, of course, we were very happy at school really. The trouble was that we were so much happier in the holidays. I have had many glorious moments since I left school, but I have no doubt as to what have been the happiest half-hours in my life. They were the half-hours on the last day of term before we started home. We spent them on a lunch of our own ordering. It was the first decent meal we had had for weeks, and when it was over there were all the holidays before us. Life may have better half-hours than that to offer, but I have not met them.

NATURAL SCIENCE

It is when Parliament is not sitting that the papers are most interesting to read. I have found an item of news to-day which would never have been given publicity in the busy times, and it has moved me strangely. Here it is, backed by the authority of Dr. Chalmers Mitchell:—

"The caterpillar of the puss-moth, not satisfied with Nature's provisions for its safety, makes faces at young birds, and is said to alarm them considreably."

I like that "is said to." Probably the young bird would deny indignantly that he was alarmed, and would explain that he was only going away because he suddenly remembered that he had an engagement on the croquet lawn, or that he had forgotten his umbrella. But whether he alarms them or not, the fact remains that the caterpillar of the puss-moth does make faces at young birds; and we may be pretty sure that, even if he began the practice in self-defence, the habit is one that has grown on him. Indeed, I can see him actually looking out for a thrush's nest, and then climbing up to it, popping his head over the edge suddenly and making a face. Probably, too, the mother birds frighten their young ones by telling them that, if they aren't good, the puss-moth caterpillar will be after them; while the poor caterpillar himself, never having known a mother's care, has had no one to tell him that if he goes on making such awful faces he will be struck like that one day.

These delvings into natural history bring back my youth very vividly. I never kept a puss-moth, but I had a goat-moth which ate its way out of a match-box, and as far as I remember took all the matches with it. There were caterpillars, though, of a gentler nature who stayed with me, and of these some were obliging enough to turn into chrysalises. Not all by any means. A caterpillar is too modest to care about changing in public. To conduct his metamorphosis in some quiet corner—where he is not poked every morning to see if he is getting stiffer —is what your caterpillar really wants. Mine had no private life to mention. They were as much before the world as royalty or an actress. And even those who brought off the first event safely never emerged into the butterfly world. Something would always happen to them. "Have you seen my chrysalis?" we used to ask each other. "I left him in the bathroom yesterday."

But what I kept most successfully were minerals. One is or is not a successful mineralogist according as one is or is not allowed a geological hammer. I had a geological hammer. To scour the cliffs armed with a geological hammer and a bag for specimens is to be a king among boys. The only specimen I can remember taking with my hammer was a small piece of shin. That was enough, however, to end my career as a successful mineralogist. As an unsuccessful one I persevered for some months, and eventually had a collection of eighteen units. They were put out on the bed every evening in order of size, and ranged from a large lump of Iceland spar down to a small dead periwinkle. In those days I could have told you what granite was made of. In those days I had over my bed a map of the geological strata of the district—in different colours like a chocolate macaroon. And in those days I knew my way to the Geological Museum.

As a botanist I never really shone, but two of us joined an open- air course and used to be taken expeditions into Kew Gardens and such places, where our lecturer explained to his pupils—all grown-up save ourselves—the less recondite mysteries. There was one golden Saturday when we missed the rendezvous at Pinner and had a picnic by ourselves instead; and, after that, many other golden Saturdays when some unaccountable accident separated us from the party. I remember particularly a day in Highgate Woods— a good place for losing a botanical lecturer in; if you had been there, you would have seen two little boys very content, lying one each side of a large stone slab, racing caterpillars against each other.

But there was one episode in my career as a natural scientist—a career whose least details are brought back by the magic word, caterpillar— over which I still go hot with the sense of failure. This was an attempt to stuff a toad. I don't know to this day if toads can be stuffed, but when our toad died he had to be commemorated in some way, and, failing a marble statue, it seemed good to stuff him. It was when we had got the skin off him that we began to realize our difficulties. I don't know if you have had the skin of a fair-sized toad in your hand; if so, you will understand that our first feeling was one of surprise that a whole toad could ever have got into it. There seemed to be no shape about the thing at all. You could have carried it—no doubt we did, I have forgotten—in the back of a watch. But it had lost all likeness to a toad, and it was obvious that stuffing meant nothing to it.

Of course, little boys ought not to skin toads and carry geological hammers and deceive learned professors of botany; I know it is wrong. And of course caterpillars of the puss-moth variety oughtn't to make faces at timid young thrushes. But it is just these things which make such pleasant memories afterwards— when professors and toads are departed, when the hammers lie rusty in the coal cellar, and when the young thrushes are grown up to be quite big birds.

ON GOING DRY

There are fortunate mortals who can always comfort themselves with a cliché. If any question arises as to the moral value of Racing, whether in war-time or in peace-time, they will murmur something about "improving the breed of horses," and sleep afterwards with an easy conscience. To one who considers how many millions of people are engaged upon this important work, it is surprising that nothing more notable in the way of a super-horse has as yet emerged; one would have expected at least by this time something which combined the flying-powers of the hawk with the diving-powers of the seal. No doubt this is what the followers of the Colonel's Late Wire are aiming at, and even if they have to borrow ten shillings from the till in the good cause, they feel that possibly by means of that very ten shillings Nature has approximated a little more closely to the desired animal. Supporters of Hunting, again, will tell you, speaking from inside knowledge, that "the fox likes it," and one is left breathless at the thought of the altruism of the human race, which will devote so much time and money to amusing a small, bushy-tailed four-legged friend who might otherwise be bored. And the third member of the Triple Alliance, which has made England what it is, is Beer, and in support of Beer there is also a cliché ready. Talk to anybody about Intemperance, and he will tell you solemnly, as if this disposed of the trouble, that "one can just as easily be intemperate in other matters as in the matter of alcohol." After which, it seems almost a duty to a broad-minded man to go out and get drunk.

It is, of course, true that we can be intemperate in eating as well as in drinking, but the results of the intemperance would appear to be different. After a fifth help of rice-pudding one does not become over-familiar with strangers, nor does an extra slice of ham inspire a man to beat his wife. After five pints of beer (or fifteen, or fifty) a man will "go anywhere in reason, but he won't go home"; after five helps of rice-pudding, I imagine, home would seem to him the one-desired haven. The two intemperances may be equally blameworthy, but they are not equally offensive to the community. Yet for some reason over- eating is considered the mark of the beast, and over-drinking the mark of rather a fine fellow.

The poets and other gentlemen who have written so much romantic nonsense about "good red wine" and "good brown ale" are responsible for this. I admit that a glass of Burgundy is a more beautiful thing than a blancmange, but I do not think that it follows that a surfeit of one is more heroic than a surfeit of the other. There may be a divinity in the grape which excuses excess, but if so, one would expect it to be there even before the grape had been trodden on by somebody else. Yet no poet ever hymned the man who tucked into the dessert, or told him that he was by way of becoming a jolly good fellow. He is only by way of becoming a pig.

"It is the true, the blushful Hippocrene." To tell oneself this is to pardon everything. However unpleasant a drunken man may seem at first sight, as soon as one realizes that he has merely been putting away a blushful Hippocrene, one ceases to be angry with him. If Keats or somebody had said of a piece of underdone mutton, "It is the true, the blushful Canterbury," indigestion would carry a more romantic air, and at the third helping one could claim to be a bit of a devil. "The beaded bubbles winking at the brim"—this might also have been sung of a tapioca- pudding, in which case a couple of tapioca- puddings would certainly qualify the recipient as one of the boys. If only the poets had praised over-eating rather than over-drinking, how much pleasanter the streets would be on festival nights!

I suppose that I have already said enough to have written myself down a Temperance Fanatic, a Thin-Blooded Cocoa-Drinker, and a number of other things equally contemptible; which is all very embarrassing to a man who is composing at the moment on port, and who gets entangled in the skin of cocoa whenever he tries to approach it. But if anything could make me take kindly to cocoa, it would be the sentimental rubbish which is written about the "manliness" of drinking alcohol. It is no more manly to drink beer (not even if you call it good brown ale) than it is to drink beef-tea. It may be more healthy; I know nothing about that, nor, from the diversity of opinion expressed, do the doctors; it may be cheaper, more thirst-quenching, anything you like. But it is a thing the village idiot can do—and often does, without becoming thereby the spiritual comrade of Robin Hood, King Harry the Fifth, Drake, and all the other heroes who (if we are to believe the Swill School) have made old England great on beer.

But to doubt the spiritual virtues of alcohol is not to be a Prohibitionist. For my own sake I want neither England nor America dry. Whether I want them dry for the sake of England and America I cannot quite decide. But if I ever do come to a decision, it will not be influenced by that other cliché, which is often trotted out complacently, as if it were something to thank Heaven for. "You can't make people moral by Act of Parliament." It is not a question of making them moral, but of keeping them from alcohol. It may be a pity to do this, but it is obviously possible, just as it is possible to keep them—that is to say, the overwhelming majority of them—from opium. Nor shall I be influenced by the argument that such prohibition is outside the authority of a Government. For if a Government can demand a man's life for reasons of foreign policy, it can surely demand his whisky for reasons of domestic policy; if it can call upon him to start fighting, it can call upon him to stop drinking.

But if opium and alcohol is prohibited, you say, why not tobacco? When tobacco is mentioned I feel like the village Socialist, who was quite ready to share two theoretical cows with his neighbour, but when asked if the theory applied also to pigs, answered indignantly, "What are you talking about—I've GOT two pigs!" I could bear an England which "went dry," but an England which "went out"—! So before assenting to the right of a Government to rob the working-man of his beer, I have to ask myself if I assent to its right to rob me of my pipe. Well, if it were agreed by a majority of the community (in spite of all my hymns to Nicotine) that England would be happier without tobacco, then I think I should agree also. But I might feel that I should be happier without England. Just a little way without—the Isle of Man, say.

A MISJUDGED GAME

Chess has this in common with making poetry, that the desire for it comes upon the amateur in gusts. It is very easy for him not to make poetry; sometimes he may go for months without writing a line of it. But when once he is delivered of an ode, then the desire to write another ode is strong upon him. A sudden passion for rhyme masters him, and must work itself out. It will be all right in a few weeks; he will go back to prose or bills-of- parcels or whatever is his natural method of expressing himself, none the worse for his adventure. But he will have gained this knowledge for his future guidance—that poems never come singly.

Every two or three years I discover the game of chess. In normal times when a man says to me, "Do you play chess?" I answer coldly, "Well, I know the moves." "Would you like a game?" he asks, and I say, "I don't think I will, thanks very much. I hardly ever play." And there the business ends. But once in two years, or it may be three, circumstances are too strong for me. I meet a man so keen or a situation so dull that politeness or boredom leads me to accept. The board is produced, I remind myself that the queen stands on a square of her own colour, and that the knight goes next to the castle; I push forward the king's pawn two squares, and we are off. Yes, we are off; but not for one game only. For a month at least I shall dream of chess at night and make excuses to play it in the day. For a month chess will be even more to me than golf or billiards— games which I adore because I am so bad at them. For a month, starting from yesterday when I was inveigled into a game, you must regard me, please, as a chess maniac.

Among small boys with no head for the game I should probably be described as a clever player. If my opponent only learnt yesterday, and is still a little doubtful as to what a knight can do, I know one or two rather good tricks for removing his queen. My subtlest

119

stroke is to wait until Her Majesty is in front of the king, and then to place my castle in front of her, with a pawn in support. Sometimes I forget the pawn and he takes my castle, in which case I try to look as if the loss of my castle was the one necessary preliminary to my plan of campaign, and that now we were off. When he is busy on one side of the board, I work a knight up on the other, and threaten two of his pieces simultaneously. To the extreme novice I must seem rather resourceful.

But then I am an old hand at the game. My career dates from—well, years ago when I won my house championship at school. This championship may have carried a belt with it; I have forgotten. But there was certainly a prize—a prize of five solid shillings, supposing the treasurer had managed to collect the subscriptions. In the year when I won it I was also treasurer. I assure you that the quickness and skill necessary for winning the competition were as nothing to that necessary for collecting the money. If any pride remains to me over that affair, if my name is written in letters of fire in the annals of our house chess club, it is because I actually obtained the five shillings.

After this the game did not trouble me for some time. But there came a day when a friend and I lunched at a restaurant in which chess-boards formed as permanent a part the furniture of the dining tables as the salt and mustard. Partly in joke, because it seemed to be the etiquette of the building, we started a game. We stayed there two hours ... and the fever remained with me for two months. Another year or so of normal development followed. Then I caught influenza and spent dull days in bed. Nothing can be worse for an influenza victim than chess, but I suppose my warders did not realize how much I suffered under the game. Anyhow, I played it all day and dreamed of it all night—a riot of games in which all the people I knew moved diagonally and up and down, took each other, and became queens.

And now I have played again, and am once more an enthusiast. You will agree with me, will you not, that it is a splendid game?

People mock at it. They say that it is not such good exercise as cricket or golf. How wrong they are. That it brings the same muscles into play as does cricket I do not claim for it. Each game develops a different set of sinews; but what chess-player who has sat with an extended forefinger on the head of his queen for five minutes, before observing the enemy's bishop in the distance and bringing back his piece to safety—what chess- player, I say, will deny that the muscles of the hand ridge up like lumps of iron after a month at the best of games? What chess-player who has stretched his arm out in order to open with the Ruy Lopez gambit, who has then withdrawn it as the possibilities of the Don Quixote occur to him, and who has finally, after another forward and backward movement, decided to rely upon the bishop's declined pawn—what chess-player, I ask, will not affirm that the biceps are elevated by this noblest of pastimes? And, finally, what chess-player, who in making too eagerly the crowning move, has upset with his elbow the victims of the preliminary skirmishing, so that they roll upon the floor- -what chess-player, who has to lean down and pick them up, will not be the better for the strain upon his diaphragm? No; say what you will against chess, but do not mock at it for its lack of exercise.

Yet there is this against it. The courtesies of the game are few. I think that this must be why the passion for it leaves me after a month. When at cricket you are bowled first ball, the wicketkeeper can comfort you by murmuring that the light is bad; when at tennis your opponent forces for the dedans and strikes you heavily under the eye, he can shout, "Sorry!" when at golf you reach a bunker in 4 and take 3 to get out, your partner can endear himself by saying, "Hard luck"; but at chess everything that the enemy does to you is deliberate. He cannot say, "Sorry!" as he takes your knight; he does not call it hard luck when your king is surrounded by vultures eager for his death; and though it would be kindly in him to attribute to the bad light the fact that you never noticed his castle leaning against your queen, yet it would be quite against the etiquette of the game.

Indeed, it is impossible to win gracefully at chess. No man yet has said "Mate!" in a voice which failed to sound to his opponent bitter, boastful, and malicious. It is the tone of that voice which, after a month, I find it impossible any longer to stand.

A DOUBTFUL CHARACTER

I find it difficult to believe in Father Christmas. If he is the jolly old gentleman he is always said to be, why doesn't he behave as such? How is it that the presents go so often to the wrong people?

This is no personal complaint; I speak for the world. The rich people get the rich presents, and the poor people get the poor ones. That may not be the fault of Father Christmas; he may be under contract for a billion years to deliver all presents just as they are addressed; but how can he go on smiling? He must long to alter all that. There is Miss Priscilla A— — who gets five guineas worth of the best every year from Mr. Cyril B— — who hopes to be her heir. Mustn't that make Father Christmas mad? Yet he goes down the chimney with it just the same. When his contract is over, and he has a free hand, he'll arrange something about THAT, I'm sure. If he is the jolly old gentleman of the pictures his sense of humour must trouble him. He must be itching to have jokes with the parcels. "Only just this once," he would plead. "Let me give Mrs. Brown the safety-razor, and Mr. Brown the night-dress case; I swear I won't touch any of the others." Of course that wouldn't be a very subtle joke; but jolly old gentlemen with white beards aren't very subtle in their humour. They lean to the broader effects—the practical joke and the pun. I can imagine Father Christmas making his annual pun on the word "reindeer," and the eldest reindeer making a feeble attempt to smile. The younger ones wouldn't so much as try. Yet he would make it so gaily that you would love him even if you couldn't laugh.

Coming down chimneys is dangerous work for white beards, and if I believed in him I should ask myself how he manages to keep so clean. I suppose his sense of humour suggested the chimney to him in the first place, and for a year or two it was the greatest joke in the world. But now he must wish sometimes that he came in by the door or the window. Some chimneys are very dirty for white beards.

Have you noticed that children, who hang up their stockings, always get lots of presents, and that we grown-ups, who don't hang up our stockings, never get any? This makes me think that perhaps after all Father Christmas has some say in the distribution. When he sees an empty stocking he pops in a few things on his own account—with "from Aunt Emma" pinned on to them. Then you write to Aunt Emma to thank her for her delightful present, and she is so ashamed of herself for not having sent you one that she never lets on about it. But when Father Christmas doesn't see a stocking, he just leaves you the embroidered tobacco pouch from your sister and the postal order from your rich uncle, and is glad to get out of the house.

Of his attitude towards Christmas cards I cannot speak with certainty, but I fancy that he does not bring these down the chimney too; the truth being, probably, that it is he who composes the mottoes on them, and that with the customary modesty of the author he leaves the distribution of them to others. "The old, old wish—a merry Christmas and a happy New Year" he considers to be his masterpiece so far, but "A righte merrie Christemasse" runs it close. "May happy hours be yours" is another epigram in the same vein which has met with considerable success. You can understand how embarrassing it would be to an author if he had to cart round his own works, and practically to force them on people. This is why you so rarely find a Christmas card in your stocking.

There is one other thing at which Father Christmas draws the line; he will not deliver venison. The reindeer say it comes too near home to them. But, apart from this, he is never so happy as when dealing with hampers. He would put a plum-pudding into every stocking if he could, for like all jolly old gentlemen with nice white beards he loves to think of people enjoying their food. I am not sure that he holds much with chocolates, although he is entrusted with so many boxes that he has learnt to look on them with kindly tolerance. But the turkey idea, I imagine (though I cannot speak with authority), the turkey idea was entirely his own. Nothing like turkey for making the beard grow.

If I believed in Father Christmas I should ask myself what he does all the summer—all the year, indeed, after his one day is over. The reindeer, of course, are put out to grass. But where is Father Christmas? Does he sleep for fifty-one weeks? Does he shave, and mix with us mortals? Or does he—yes, that must be it- -does he spend the year in training, in keeping down his figure? Chimney work is terribly trying; the figure wants watching if one is to carry it through successfully. This is especially so in the case of jolly old gentlemen with white beards. I can see Father Christmas, as soon as his day is over, taking himself off to the Equator and running round and round it. By next December he is in splendid condition.

When his billion years are over, when his contract expires and he is allowed a free hand with the presents, I suppose I shall not be alive to take part in the distribution. But none the less I like to think of the things I should get. There are at least half a dozen things which I deserve, and Father Christmas knows it. In any equitable scheme of allotment I should come out well. "Half a minute," he would say, "I must just put these cigars aside for the gentleman who had the picture post card last year. What have you got there? The country cottage and the complete edition of Meredith? Ah yes, perhaps he'd better have those too."

That would be something like a Father Christmas.

THOUGHTS ON THERMOMETERS

Our thermometer went down to 11 deg. the other night. The excitement was intense. It was, of course, the first person down to breakfast who rushed into the garden and made the discovery, and as each of us appeared he was greeted with the news.

"I say, do you know there were twenty-one degrees of frost last night?"

"Really? By Jove!"

We were all very happy and talkative at breakfast—an event rare enough to be chronicled. It was not that we particularly wanted a frost, but that we felt that, if it was going to freeze, it might as well do it properly—so as to show other nations that England was still to be reckoned with. And there was also the feeling that if the thermometer could get down to 11 deg. it might some day get down to zero; and then perhaps the Thames would be frozen over again at Westminster, and the papers would be full of strange news, and—generally speaking—life would be a little different from the ordinary. In a word, there would be a chance of something "happening"— which, I take it, is why one buys a thermometer and watches it so carefully.

Of course, every nice thermometer has a device for registering the maximum and minimum temperatures, which can only be set with a magnet. This gives you an opportunity of using a magnet in ordinary life, an opportunity which occurs all too seldom. Indeed, I can think of no other occasion on which it plays any important part in one's affairs. It would be interesting to know if the sale of magnets exceeds the sale of thermometers, and if so, why?—and it would also be interesting to know why magnets are always painted red, as if they were dangerous, or belonged to the Government, or—but this is a question into which it is impossible to go now. My present theme is thermometers.

Our thermometer (which went down to 11 deg. the other night) is not one of your common mercury ones; it is filled with a pink fluid which I am told is alcohol, though I have never tried. It hangs in the kitchen garden. This gives you an excuse in summer for going into the kitchen garden and leaning against the fruit trees. "Let's go and look at the thermometer" you say to your guest from London, and just for the moment he thinks that the amusements of the country are not very dramatic. But after a day or two he learns that what you really mean is, "Let's go and see if any fruit has blown down in the night." And he takes care to lean against the right tree. An elaborate subterfuge, but necessary if your gardener is at all strict.

But whether your thermometer hangs in the kitchen garden or at the back of the shrubbery, you must recognize one thing about it, namely, that it is an open-air plant. There are people who keep thermometers shut up indoors, which is both cruel and unnecessary. When you complain that the library is a little chilly— as surely you are entitled to—they look at the thermometer nailed to the Henry Fielding shelf and say, "Oh no; I don't think so. It's sixty-five." As if anybody wanted a thermometer to know if a room were cold or not. These people insult thermometers and their guests further by placing one of the former in the bathroom soap-dish, in order that the latter may discover whether it is a hot or cold bath which they are having. All decent people know that a hot bath is one which you can just bear to get into, and that a cold bath is one which you cannot bear to think of getting into, but have to for honour's sake. They do riot want to be told how many degrees Fahrenheit it is.

The undersized temperature-taker which the doctor puts under your tongue before telling you to keep warm and take plenty of milk puddings is properly despised by every true thermometer-lover. Any record which it makes is too personal for a breakfast-table topic, and moreover it is a thermometer which affords no scope for the magnet. Altogether it is a contemptible thing. An occasional devotee will bite it in two before returning it to its owner, but this is rather a strong line to take. It is perhaps best to avoid it altogether by not being ill.

A thermometer must always be treated with care, for the mercury once spilt can only be replaced with great difficulty. It is considered to be one of the most awkward things to pick up after dinner, and only a very steady hand will be successful. Some people with a gift for handling mercury or alcohol make their own thermometers; but even when you have got the stuff into the tube, it is always a question where to put the little figures. So much depends upon them.

Now I must tell you the one hereditary failing of the thermometer. I had meant to hide it from you, but I see that you are determined to have it. It is this: you cannot go up to it and tap it. At least you can, but you don't get that feeling of satisfaction from it which the tapping of a barometer gives you. Of course you can always put a hot thumb on the bulb and watch the mercury run up; this is satisfying for a short time, but it is not the same thing as tapping. And I am wrong to say "always," for in some thermometers— indeed, in ours, alas!—the bulb is wired in, so that no falsifying thumb can get to work. However, this has its compensations, for if no hot thumb can make our thermometer untrue to itself, neither can any cold thumb. And so when I tell you again that our thermometer did go down to 11 deg. the other night, you have no excuse for not believing that our twenty-one degrees of frost was a genuine affair. In fact, you will appreciate our excitement at breakfast.

FOR A WET AFTERNOON

Let us consider something seasonable; let us consider indoor games for a moment.

And by indoor games I do not mean anything so serious as bridge and billiards, nor anything so commercial as vingt-et-un with fish counters, nor anything so strenuous as "bumps." The games I mean are those jolly, sociable ones in which everybody in the house can join with an equal chance of distinction, those friendly games which are played with laughter round a fire what time the blizzards rattle against the window-pane.

These games may be divided broadly into two classes; namely, paper games and guessing games. The initial disadvantage of the paper game is that pencils have to be found for everybody; generally a difficult business. Once they are found, there is no further trouble until the game is over, when the pencils have to be collected from everybody; generally an impossible business. If you are a guest in the house, insist upon a paper game, for it gives you a chance of acquiring a pencil; if you are the host, consider carefully whether you would not rather play a guessing game.

But the guessing game has one great disadvantage too. It demands periodically that a member of the company should go out by himself into the hall and wait there patiently until his companions have "thought of something." (It may be supposed that he, too, is thinking of something in the cold hall, but perhaps not liking to say it.) However careful the players are, unpleasantness is bound to arise sometimes over this preliminary stage of the game. I knew of one case where the people in the room forgot all about the lady waiting in the hall and began to tell each other ghost stories. The lights were turned out, and sitting round the flickering fire the most imaginative members of the household thrilled their hearers with ghostly tales of the dead. Suddenly, in the middle of the story of Torfrida of the Towers—a lady who had strangled her children, and ever afterwards haunted the battlements, headless, and in a night-gown—the door opened softly, and Miss Robinson entered to ask how much longer they would be. Miss Robinson was wearing a white frock, and the effect of her entry was tremendous. I remember, too, another evening when we were playing "proverbs." William, who had gone outside, was noted for his skill at the game, and we were determined to give him something difficult; something which hadn't a camel or a glass house or a stable door in it. After some discussion a member of the company suggested a proverb from the Persian, as he alleged. It went something like this: "A wise man is kind to his dog, but a poor man riseth early in the morning." We took his word for it, and, feeling certain that William would never guess, called him to come in.

Unfortunately William, who is a trifle absentminded, had gone to bed.

To avoid accidents of this nature it is better to play "clumps," a guessing game in which the procedure is slightly varied. In "clumps" two people go into the hall and think of something, while the rest remain before the fire. Thus, however long the interval of waiting, all are happy; for the people inside can tell each other stories (or, as a last resort, play some other game) and the two outside are presumably amusing themselves in arranging something very difficult. Personally I adore clumps; not only for this reason, but because of its revelation of hidden talent. There may be a dozen persons in each clump, and in theory every one of the dozen is supposed to take a hand in the cross- examination, but in practice it is always one person who extracts the information required by a cataract of searching questions. Always one person and generally a girl. I love to see her coming out of her shell. She has excelled at none of the outdoor games perhaps; she has spoken hardly a word at meals. In our little company she has scarcely seemed to count. But suddenly she awakes into life. Clumps is the family game at home; she has been brought up on it. In a moment she discovers herself as our natural leader, a leader whom we follow humbly. And however we may spend the rest of our time together, the effect of her short hour's triumph will not wholly wear away. She is now established.

But the paper games will always be most popular, and once you are over the difficulty of the pencils you may play them for hours without wearying. But of course you must play the amusing ones and not the dull ones. The most common paper game of all, that of making small words out of a big one, has nothing to recommend it; for there can be no possible amusement in hearing somebody else read out "but," "bat," "bet," "bin," "ben," and so forth, riot even if you spend half an hour discussing whether "ben" is really a word. On the other hand your game, however amusing, ought to have some finality about it; a game is not really a game unless somebody can win it. For this reason I cannot wholly approve "telegrams." To concoct a telegram whose words begin with certain selected letters of the alphabet, say the first ten, is to amuse yourself anyhow and possibly your friends; whether you say, "Am bringing camel down early Friday. Got hump. Inform Jamrach"; or, "Afraid better cancel dinner engagement. Fred got horrid indigestion.—JANE." But it is impossible to declare yourself certainly the winner. Fortunately, however, there are games which combine amusement with a definite result; games in which the others can be funny while you can get the prize—or, if you prefer it, the other way about.

When I began to write this, the rain was streaming against the window-panes. It is now quite fine. This, you will notice, often happens when you decide to play indoor games on a wet afternoon. Just as you have found the pencils, the sun comes out.

DECLINED WITH THANKS

A paragraph in the papers of last week recorded the unusual action of a gentleman called Smith (or some such name) who had refused for reasons of conscience to be made a justice of the peace. Smith's case was that the commission was offered to him as a reward for political services, and that this was a method of selecting magistrates of which he did not approve. So he showed his contempt for the system by refusing an honour which most people covet, and earned by this such notoriety as the papers can give. "Portrait (on page 8) of a gentleman who has refused something!" He takes his place with Brittlebones in the gallery of freaks.

The subject for essay has frequently been given, "If a million pounds were left to you, how could you do most good with it?" Some say they would endow hospitals, some that they would establish almshouses; there may even be some who would go as far as to build half a Dreadnought. But there would be a more decisive way of doing good than any of these. You might refuse the million pounds. That would be a shock to the systems of the comfortable — a blow struck at the great Money God which would make it totter; a thrust in defence of pride and freedom such as had not been seen before. That would be a moral tonic more needed than all the draughts of your newly endowed hospitals. Will it ever be administered? Well, perhaps when the D.W.T. club has grown a little stronger.

Have you heard of the D.W.T.—the Declined- with-Thanks Club? There are no club rooms and not many members, but the balance sheet for the last twelve months is wonderful, showing that more than £11,000 was refused. The entrance fee is one hundred guineas and the annual subscription fifty guineas; that is to say, you must have refused a hundred guineas before you can be elected, and you are expected to refuse another fifty guineas a year while you retain membership. It is possible also to compound with a life refusal, but the sum is not fixed, and remains at the discretion of the committee.

Baines is a life member. He saved an old lady from being run over by a motor bus some years ago, and when she died she left him a legacy of £1000. Baines wrote to the executors and pointed out that he did not go about dragging persons from beneath motor buses as a profession; that, if she had offered him £1000 at the time, he would have refused it, not being in the habit of accepting money from strangers, still less from women; and that he did not see that the fact of the money being offered two years later in a will made the slightest difference. Baines was earning £300 a year at this time, and had a wife and four children, but he will not admit that he did anything at all out of the common.

The case of Sedley comes up for consideration at the next committee meeting. Sedley's rich uncle, a cantankerous old man, insulted him grossly; there was a quarrel; and the old man left, vowing to revenge himself by disinheriting his nephew and bequeathing his money to a cats' home. He died on his way to his solicitors, and Sedley was told of his good fortune in good legal English. He replied, "What on earth do you take me for? I wouldn't touch a penny. Give it to the cats' home or any blessed thing you like." Sedley, of course, will be elected as an ordinary member, but as there is a strong feeling on the committee that no decent man could have done anything else, his election as a life member is improbable.

Though there are one or two other members like Baines and Sedley, most of them are men who have refused professional openings rather than actual money. There are, for instance, half a dozen journalists and authors. Now a journalist, before he can be elected, must have a black-list of papers for which he will refuse to write. A concocted wireless message in the Daily Blank, which subsequent events proved to have been invented deliberately for the purpose of raking in ha'pennies, so infuriated Henderson (to take a case) that he has pledged himself never to write a line for any paper owned by the same proprietors. Curiously enough he was asked a day or two later to contribute a series to a most respectable magazine published by this firm. He refused in a letter which breathed hatred and utter contempt in every word. It was Henderson, too, who resigned his position as dramatic critic because the proprietor of his paper did rather a shady thing in private life. "I know the paper isn't mixed up in it at all," he said, "but he's my employer and he pays me. Well, I like to be loyal to my employers, and if I'm loyal to this man I can't go about telling everybody that he's a dirty cad. As I particularly want to."

Then there is the case of Bolus the author. He is only an honorary member, for he has not as yet had the opportunity of refusing money or work. But he has refused to be photographed and interviewed, and he has refused to contribute to symposia in the monthly magazines. He has declined with thanks, moreover, invitations to half a dozen houses sent to him by hostesses who only knew him by reputation. Myself, I think it is time that he was elected a full member; indirectly he must have been a financial loser by his action, and even if he is not actually assisting to topple over the Money God, he is at least striking a blow for the cause of independence. However, there he is, and with him goes a certain M.P. who contributed £20,000 to the party chest, and refused scornfully the peerage which was offered to him.

The Bar is represented by P. J. Brewster, who was elected for refusing to defend a suspected murderer until he had absolutely convinced himself of the man's innocence. It was suggested to him by his legal brothers that counsel did not pledge themselves to the innocence of their clients, but merely put the case for one side in a perfectly detached way, according to the best traditions of the Bar. Brewster replied that he was also quite capable of putting the case for Tariff Reform in a perfectly detached way according to the best traditions of The Morning Post, but as he was a Free Trader he thought he would refuse any such offer if it were made to him. He added, however, that he was not in the present case worrying about moral points of view; he was simply expressing his opinion that the luxury of not having little notes passed to him in court by a probable murderer, of not sharing a page in an illustrated paper with him, and of not having to shake hands with him if he were acquitted, was worth paying for. Later on, when as K.C., M.P., he refused the position of standing counsel to a paper which he was always attacking in the House, he became a life member of the club.

But it would be impossible to mention all the members of the D.W.T. by name. I have been led on to speaking about the club by the mention of that Mr. Smith (or whatever his name was) who refused to be made a justice of the peace. If Mr. Smith cared to put up as an honorary member, I have no doubt that he would be elected; for though it is against the Money God that the chief battle is waged, yet the spirit of refusal is the same. "Blessed are they who know how to refuse," runs the club's motto, "for they will have a chance to be clean."

ON GOING INTO A HOUSE

It is nineteen years since I lived in a house; nineteen years since I went upstairs to bed and came downstairs to breakfast. Of course I have done these things in other people's houses from time to time, but what we do in other people's houses does not count. We are holiday-making then. We play cricket and golf and croquet, and run up and down stairs, and amuse ourselves in a hundred different ways, but all this is no fixed part of our life. Now, however, for the first time for nineteen years, I am actually living in a house. I have (imagine my excitement) a staircase of my own.

Flats may be convenient (I thought so myself when I lived in one some days ago), but they have their disadvantages. One of the disadvantages is that you are never in complete possession of the flat. You may think that the drawing-room floor (to take a case) is your very own, but it isn't; you share it with a man below who uses it as a ceiling. If you want to dance a step-dance, you have to consider his plaster. I was always ready enough to accommodate myself in this matter to his prejudices, but I could not put up with his old-fashioned ideas about bathroom ceilings. It is very cramping to one's style in the bath to reflect that the slightest splash may call attention to itself on the ceiling of the gentleman below. This is to share a bathroom with a stranger—an intolerable position for a proud man. To-day I have a bathroom of my own for the first time in my life.

I can see already that living in a house is going to be extraordinarily healthy both for mind and body. At present I go upstairs to my bedroom (and downstairs again) about once in every half-hour; not simply from pride of ownership, to make sure that the bedroom is still there, and that the staircase is continuing to perform its functions, but in order to fetch something, a letter or a key, which as likely as not I have forgotten about again as soon as I have climbed to the top of the house. No such exercise as this was possible in a flat, and even after two or three days I feel the better for it. But obviously I cannot go on like this, if I am to have leisure for anything else. With practice I shall so train my mind that, when I leave my bedroom in the morning, I leave it with everything that I can possibly require until nightfall. This, I imagine, will not happen for some years yet; meanwhile physical training has precedence.

Getting up to breakfast means something different now; it means coming down to breakfast. To come down to breakfast brings one immediately in contact with the morning. The world flows past the window, that small and (as it seems to me) particularly select portion of the world which finds itself in our quiet street; I can see it as I drink my tea. When I lived in a flat (days and days ago) anything might have happened to London, and I should never have known it until the afternoon. Everybody else could have perished in the night, and I should settle down as complacently as ever to my essay on making the world safe for democracy. Not so now. As soon as I have reached the bottom of my delightful staircase I am one with the outside world.

Also one with the weather, which is rather convenient. On the third floor it is almost impossible to know what sort of weather they are having in London. A day which looks cold from a third- floor window may be very sultry down below, but by that time one is committed to an overcoat. How much better to live in a house, and to step from one's front door and inhale a sample of whatever day the gods have sent. Then one can step back again and dress accordingly.

But the best of a house is that it has an outside personality as well as an inside one. Nobody, not even himself, could admire a man's flat from the street; nobody could look up and say, "What very delightful people must live behind those third-floor windows." Here it is different. Any of you may find himself some day in our quiet street, and stop a moment to look at our house; at the blue door with its jolly knocker, at the little trees in their blue tubs standing within a ring of blue posts linked by chains, at the bright-coloured curtains. You may not like it, but we shall be watching you from one of the windows, and telling each other that you do. In any case, we have the pleasure of looking at it ourselves, and feeling that we are contributing something to London, whether for better or for worse. We are part of a street now, and can take pride in that street. Before, we were only part of a big unmanageable building. It is a solemn thought that I have got this house for (apparently) eighty-seven years. One never knows, and it may be that by the end of that time I shall be meditating an article on the advantages of living in a flat. A flat, I shall say, is so convenient.

THE IDEAL AUTHOR

Samuel Butler made a habit (and urged it upon every young writer) of carrying a notebook about with him. The most profitable ideas, he felt, do not come from much seeking, but rise unbidden in the mind, and if they are not put down at once on paper, they may be lost for ever. But with a notebook in the pocket you are safe; no thought is too fleeting to escape you. Thus, if an inspiration for a five-thousand word story comes suddenly to you during the dessert, you murmur an apology to your neighbour, whip out your pocket-book, and jot down a few rough notes. "Hero choked peach-stone eve marriage Lady Honoria. Pchtree planted by jltd frst love. Ironyofthings. Tragic." Next morning you extract your notebook from its white waistcoat, and prepare to develop your theme (if legible) a little more fully. Possibly it does not seem so brilliant in the cold light of morning as it did after that fourth glass of Bollinger. If this be so, you can then make another note—say, for a short article on "Disillusionment." One way or another a notebook and a pencil will keep you well supplied with material.

If I do not follow Butler's advice myself, it is not because I get no brilliant inspirations away from my inkpot, nor because, having had the inspirations, I am capable of retaining them until I get back to my inkpot again, but simply because I should never have the notebook and the pencil in the right pockets. But though I do not imitate him, I can admire his wisdom, even while making fun of it. Yet I am sure it was unwise of him to take the public into his confidence. The public prefers to think that an author does not require these earthly aids to composition. It will never quite reconcile itself to the fact that an author is following a profession— a profession by means of which he pays the rent and settles the weekly bills. No doubt the public wants its favourite writers to go on living, but not in the sordid way that its barrister and banker

139

friends live. It would prefer to feel that manna dropped on them from Heaven, and that the ravens erected them a residence; but, having regretfully to reject this theory, it likes to keep up the pretence that the thousand pounds that an author received for his last story came as something of a surprise to him—being, in fact, really more of a coincidence than a reward.

The truth is that a layman will never take an author quite seriously. He regards authorship, not as a profession, but as something between au inspiration and a hobby. In as far as it is an inspiration, it is a gift from Heaven, and ought, therefore, to be shared with the rest of the world; in as far as it is a hobby, it is something which should be done not too expertly, but in a casual, amateur, haphazard fashion. For this reason a layman will never hesitate to ask of an author a free contribution for some local publication, on such slender grounds as that he and the author were educated at the same school or had both met Robinson. But the same man would be horrified at the idea of asking a Harley Street surgeon (perhaps even more closely connected with him) to remove his adenoids for nothing. To ask for this (he would feel) would be almost as bad as to ask a gift of ten guineas (or whatever the fee is), whereas to ask a writer for an article is like asking a friend to decant your port for you—a delicate compliment to his particular talent. But in truth the matter is otherwise; and it is the author who has the better right to resent such a request. For the supply of available adenoids is limited, and if the surgeon hesitates to occupy himself in removing one pair for nothing, it does not follow that in the time thus saved he can be certain of getting employment upon a ten-guinea pair. But when a Harley Street author has written an article, there are a dozen papers which will give him his own price for it, and if he sends it to his importunate schoolfellow for nothing, he is literally giving up, not only ten or twenty or a hundred guineas, but a publicity for his work which he may prize even more highly. Moreover, he has lost what can never be replaced— an idea; whereas the surgeon would have lost nothing.

Since, then, the author is not to be regarded as a professional, he must by no means adopt the professional notebook. He is to write by inspiration; which comes as regularly to him (it is to be presumed) as indigestion to a lesser-favoured mortal. He must know things by intuition; not by experience or as the result of reading. This, at least, is what one gathers from hearing some people talk about our novelists. The hero of Smith's new book goes to the Royal College of Science, and the public says scornfully: "Of course, he WOULD. Because Smith went to the Royal College himself, all his heroes have to go there. This isn't art, this is photography." In his next novel Smith sends his hero to Cambridge, and the public says indignantly, "What the deuce does SMITH know about Cambridge? Trying to pretend he is a 'Varsity man, when everybody knows that he went to the Royal College of Science! I suppose he's been mugging it up in a book." Perhaps Brown's young couple honeymoons in Switzerland. "So did Brown," sneer his acquaintances. Or they go to Central Africa. "How ridiculous," say his friends this time. "Why, he actually writes as though he'd been there! I suppose he's just spent a week-end with Sir Harry Johnston." Meredith has been blamed lately for being so secretive about his personal affairs, but he knew what he was doing. Happy is the writer who has no personal affairs; at any rate, he will avoid this sort of criticism.

Indeed, Isaiah was the ideal author. He intruded no private affairs upon the public. He took no money for his prophecies, and yet managed to live on it. He responded readily, I imagine, to any request for "something prophetic, you know," from acquaintances or even strangers. Above all, he kept to one style, and did not worry the public, when once it had got used to him, by tentative gropings after a new method. And Isaiah, we may be sure, did NOT carry a notebook.

End of Not That it Matters

www.ingramcontent.com/pod-product-compliance
Lightning Source LLC
Chambersburg PA
CBHW020140180626
46810CB00004B/1651